The Christmas Magpie

Also by Mark Edwards

The Magpies Series

The Magpies
A Murder of Magpies
Last of the Magpies
The Psychopath Next Door

Other Novels

What You Wish For
Because She Loves Me
Follow You Home
The Devil's Work
The Lucky Ones
The Retreat
In Her Shadow
Here To Stay
The House Guest
The Hollows
No Place To Run
Keep Her Secret
The Darkest Water
The Wasp Trap

With Louise Voss

Killing Cupid
Catch Your Death
All Fall Down
Forward Slash
From the Cradle
The Blissfully Dead

The Christmas Magpie

MARK EDWARDS

MICHAEL JOSEPH

PENGUIN MICHAEL JOSEPH

UK | USA | Canada | Ireland | Australia
India | New Zealand | South Africa

Penguin Michael Joseph is part of the Penguin Random House group of companies
whose addresses can be found at global.penguinrandomhouse.com

Penguin Random House UK,
One Embassy Gardens, 8 Viaduct Gardens, London SW11 7BW

penguin.co.uk

Penguin
Random House
UK

First published 2025

001

Set in 13.5/16pt Garamond MT
Typeset by Falcon Oast Graphic Art Ltd
Printed and bound in Great Britain by Clays Ltd, Elcograf S.p.A.

The authorized representative in the EEA is Penguin Random House Ireland,
Morrison Chambers, 32 Nassau Street, Dublin D02 YH68

A CIP catalogue record for this book is available from the British Library

ISBN: 978-0-241-78902-5

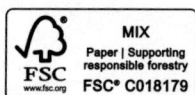

MIX
Paper | Supporting
responsible forestry
FSC® C018179

For my sister, Claire

I

The first parcel was waiting on the doorstep when Noel got home from work. It was the beginning of December and a chill hung in the air, the faintest promise of snow, although Noel wasn't quite *that* optimistic. He was thirty years old and had never experienced a white Christmas, but if it did happen this year it would be the almost-literal icing on the cake. Because Noel had already decided that this was going to be the best Christmas ever.

He picked the parcel up. It was the shape, size and approximate weight of a large box of chocolates, wrapped in shiny red paper with a pattern of gold holly leaves. A matching red ribbon was tied around it. He shook it gently and read the gift tag that was attached to it, handwritten in block capitals.

A little something to welcome you to the neighbourhood. Love, Secret Santa x

This was a lovely surprise, but who could be responsible? He looked up and down the street.

Nightingale Crescent, named after the famous nurse rather than the bird, was curved liked a rainbow, and Noel and Dani's house was right in the middle. The street was part of a development that was less than a decade old, located several miles outside Telford in Shropshire, all the roads named after famous Brits: Churchill, Turing, Elizabeth Fry. The lights were on in most of the houses, although no one had put their decorations up already. They were all too afraid of upsetting Linda, the chairperson of the residents' association, who lived with her husband at the end of the crescent.

Linda had come to greet Noel and Dani the day they'd moved in, just three weeks ago, while they were still unpacking. Linda was in her mid-fifties, with auburn hair cut into a bob, and Noel wasn't at all surprised to learn she was the principal of a nearby selective girls' school.

'It's so lovely to see a young couple move in,' Linda had said, inviting herself in and waving away Dani's apology that she couldn't offer her a cup of tea because they had yet to locate the kettle. 'There are too many old crusties like me and Alan – that's my husband – around here. How long have you two been together, if you don't mind me asking?'

'Three years,' Noel had replied.

'And were you living together before this?'

Dani had answered that one. 'Only for six months. I was renting a flat in Telford and Noel moved in after my flatmate went to live with her boyfriend.'

'A trial run. Sensible. So this is your first Christmas living together?'

Noel reached out to squeeze Dani's hand. 'It is. I've been looking forward to it all year.'

Linda beamed. 'How exciting. Well, we are thrilled to have you. This community is perfect for families and we simply don't have enough.'

She had waited expectantly and Noel had been unable to resist filling the silence.

'We're hoping to start one soon.'

'Oh, that's marvellous. A future Brookes High girl, perhaps.' She had winked at them. 'I remember when Alan and I got married and moved in together. Our first little nest. Such a wonderful time.' A big sigh. 'This is such a perfect time to move in too, with Christmas just around the corner, I mean. We fully embrace the festive season here. Um . . . assuming you celebrate Christmas?'

'How could I not,' Noel said, 'with a name like mine?'

She clapped her hands together, as if she'd just

seen one of her Brookes High girls do something *marvellous*. 'Let me guess – born on the twenty-fifth?'

'The twenty-fourth. If I'd been a girl my parents would have called me Eve.'

'*Love* it. You've made a wonderful choice moving here. We're trying to ensure this is a proper community, not just a collection of strangers who happen to live near each other. Neighbours looking out for each other. It's a lovely part of the world too, even if—'

'What?' Dani had asked.

'I feel bad saying it, especially as I fully believe in rehabilitation. It's why I pushed for one of the streets here to be named after Elizabeth Fry.'

Noel hadn't heard that name before moving here but, as Elizabeth Fry Way was the next street along, he'd looked her up. She had been a women's prison reformer in the nineteenth century.

'You're talking about the prison?'

Linda had pursed her lips. 'Yes. Franklin Grange. I'm sure you're aware it's only a few miles up the road.'

'It's an open prison, isn't it?' Dani asked. 'White-collar criminals and women who are about to finish their sentences?'

4

'Mostly.' Again, Linda cleared her throat. 'Anyway, I should let you get on. You need to find that kettle. By the way, I know it's a few weeks away, but regarding Christmas, the whole neighbourhood has a big switch-on ceremony the first Saturday of December. We encourage everyone to decorate the exterior of their houses. Fairy lights in the trees, wreaths on the front door, that kind of thing. I can tell from looking at the pair of you that you're the type that prefers tasteful decorations. White lights. No ghastly flashing Santas on the roof or gaudy, bright colours.' She shuddered. 'Alan and I have prepared a little guide, in fact. I'll pop a copy through your letterbox.'

Noel had been taken aback. 'Um, thanks.'

'Don't mention it. Again, welcome to the neighbourhood.' A wink. 'Have fun christening the place.'

After Linda had left, Dani had burst out laughing. 'A guide? Telling us how to tastefully decorate our house?'

'I don't think it's a bad idea. If it helps make the whole street look — what do they say on TikTok? Aesthetic.'

Dani worked as a social media manager for a marketing agency in Telford and spent most of her workday on TikTok and Instagram. It was how they'd met: Noel worked for a company that managed several local tourist attractions, and they had hired Dani's firm to run a campaign for them. That had been three years ago, and Noel still couldn't believe his luck. The first time he'd seen her, he'd caught his breath. He'd never experienced instant attraction like that, and he'd spent the next few weeks trying to gather the courage to ask her on a date, convinced she would say no, and finding excuses to visit her office for meetings to discuss the project. It turned out she'd been about to ask him out herself, fed up with the tension and the teasing from her best friend at work, Zoe.

'Also,' Dani had continued, 'why did you tell her we're planning to start a family?'

'Well, we are, aren't we?'

'Yes, I know, but . . . you're such an over-sharer. Also, didn't you think it's slightly concerning that she seemed so keen on the idea of us having kids?' She dropped her voice to a theatrical whisper. '*Oh, how lovely. A baby. Our Satanic cult is always in need of fresh blood.*'

'Dani!'

'Come on, it did seem a bit *Rosemary's Baby*. If she gives me a necklace containing some dubious, stinky herb to wear I'm putting the house on the market.'

They had laughed together, then continued their hunt for the kettle. Later, when all the weird stuff started to happen, Noel would think back to this exchange. But that night, they had got a take-away and watched a movie on Dani's laptop. Not a horror film, though. *Love Actually*. Noel had only seen it, ooh, fifty times before. And afterwards, he and Dani had made love right there on the floor of their living room, laughing together about Linda's comment: *Christening the place*.

They had only been in the house a few hours, but it already felt like home.

2

Now, Noel went inside, taking the parcel with him and setting it on the counter in the kitchen. He didn't want to open it until Dani got home.

The house was small, a starter home with two bedrooms, although it also had a basement, and there was something a little modern about it that had initially put him off buying it. Noel preferred old places, homes with history, stories imprinted in the walls. But Dani had made it clear that she would never be able to live somewhere like that. Old houses reminded her too much of the incident that had terrified her when she was a little girl. 'Do you want me to have bad dreams every night?' she had asked, when he'd suggested looking at a Victorian fixer-upper down a dark country lane.

Of course he didn't. Her happiness trumped everything, and it was all fine because, despite being close to town, this place was surrounded by countryside. There was a playing field on the north side of the estate and, beyond that, woods that sprawled in every direction.

It was a shame they didn't have a dog, Noel thought. It wouldn't be fair for them to get one, with both of them working. They did, though, have a cat, an enormous fluffy Maine Coone called Mogwai. She came padding into the kitchen now, leaping on to the kitchen counter and emitting the chirruping noise that Noel found so adorable. After allowing him to stroke her, she approached the parcel and sniffed it, recoiling instantly and jumping down to the floor, her tail puffed up.

'I'm guessing it's not a roast chicken, then,' he said.

He fed her, then sat at the counter and opened his laptop. He had done a lot of his Christmas shopping already, but he kept thinking of things Dani might like. He intended to thoroughly spoil her this year – even though she kept pointing out they weren't rolling in cash. Every penny they had saved had gone on the deposit for this place.

He had, though, unknown to Dani, squirrelled away a few hundred pounds for presents. As well as Dani's gifts, he needed to send something to his niece and nephew, who lived with his sister in Kent. He was browsing a toy site when he heard

Dani's car pull up outside and, shortly afterwards, her key in the front door. Mogwai ran out to greet her.

He kissed her hello and her eyes fell on the parcel on the counter.

'What's this?' She picked it up and read the label. 'Secret Santa? Oh no, is that some neighbourhood scheme we're supposed to take part in? Did we miss a memo from Linda?'

That hadn't crossed Noel's mind. 'I think it's just a present for us. One of the neighbours being sweet. I was waiting for you to get home before opening it.'

'Don't you think we should wait until Christmas Day?'

'Why? It's a "welcome to the neighbourhood" gift. I'm going to open it now.'

He tried to take it from her, knowing she wouldn't let him. She often accused him of being a big kid, but she loved presents as much as he did. Setting it back down on the counter, she untied the ribbon and ripped off the wrapping paper. Inside was a plain cardboard box with a lid. She lifted it to reveal the contents.

'Mince pies.'

Noel noticed Mogwai standing in the kitchen

doorway, her back arched. She was a house cat, too daft to be allowed outside, and because she never encountered other animals he hadn't seen her like this before. She was acting like a pet in a horror movie, when an evil spirit the humans can't detect enters the room.

'I don't think Mogwai is a fan of mince pies,' Noel said, taking one out of the box. They were clearly home-baked, the pastry thick and flaky, with a dusting of sugar on the top. 'I, on the other hand . . .'

He bit into the pie. Immediately, his mouth filled with saliva, his taste buds yelling at him, a burning sensation filling his nose. He ran to the bin and spat everything into it, then crossed to the sink and ran his mouth under the cold tap, spitting water that still contained traces of the mincemeat and pastry.

'What is it?' Dani stared at him.

'It's hot!' He took another mouthful of water and rinsed his mouth out. His tongue burned like he'd just eaten a Scotch bonnet chilli.

Dani split open one of the other pies. Tentatively, she sniffed it, then touched one half against her tongue. 'Urgh, you're not kidding.'

He must have looked so disgusted that Dani laughed.

'Do you think this is someone's idea of a prank?' he asked.

'It's a pretty weird one if it is. I think it's more likely that someone got their cinnamon and chilli powder mixed up.'

'Really?'

'Remember that time you put salt in my tea?'

'That was because your housemate kept everything in mislabelled jars! Anyway, cinnamon and chilli powder are different colours.'

'I know, but . . .' She paused. 'It was a probably a kid. Either a mistake or a prank.

'I wish I'd videoed you biting into that pie. I could have used it in this TikTok campaign we're running.'

'I'm glad you find it so hilarious.' He grabbed hold of her and pulled her close. 'Here, give me a kiss.'

'Urgh, get off, chilli face.' She laughed and pulled away. 'I'm going to take a shower.'

She left Noel in the kitchen, looking out of the window at the houses across the street. Had it really been a baking mishap? He imagined that soon someone would ask him if he'd enjoyed the mince pies and he'd have to decide whether to be honest. *Er, no, it nearly burned the roof of my mouth off.*

But what if it *was* a prank? A stupid practical joke? One of the few kids or teenagers in the neighbourhood, easing their suburban boredom. It was the kind of thing some of his old mates at uni might have done, thinking it was hilarious. But what was the point of a prank when you couldn't see the reaction of the victim?

Yes, it probably was an honest mistake. And if it wasn't? Well, he hoped it had been kids. Because for a fully grown adult to pull a stunt like that, you wouldn't just have to be immature or stupid.

You'd need to have something seriously wrong with you.

3

It was the evening of the big Christmas lights switch-on. Saturday, 7 December, at least a week later than Noel usually put his decorations up. Linda had gone door to door a week ago to remind everyone that if they wanted to take part (and she very much hoped they would, though no pressure), they would need to put their outdoor lights up in the next few days. She had messaged the neighbourhood WhatsApp group multiple times too.

The fun kicks off at 5pm with the big Switch-On happening at 6. So exciting! Let me or Alan (hubby) know if you need any help!

There had followed an explosion of emojis: a Christmas tree, a snowman, Santa, a party hat and a star, followed by a row of houses.

It amused Noel that whenever Linda mentioned Alan she had to remind everyone he was her husband, as if he was so unmemorable that she expected a flurry of replies asking who he was.

Linda and Alan were standing outside their house at the end of Nightingale Crescent now, in front of a pine tree that was so big it looked like it must have been gifted to the people of the UK by some Scandinavian royal. The tree was strung with fairy lights – white ones, of course – which were yet to be turned on, and the house and front garden were festooned with similar tasteful decorations: a lush wreath that hung on the front door, a family of prancing wire reindeer on the lawn, more lights just beneath the guttering, and a large five-pointed star on the front wall. 'See,' said Dani, nudging Noel and whispering in his ear. 'A pentagram.'

All the houses on the street, and the adjoining streets on the development, were decorated in a similar fashion. In her messages, Linda had made it clear this was a holiday celebration, a chance for everyone here to help dispel the winter darkness, so, whatever your faith, it would be 'absolutely marvellous' if everyone joined in.

As far as Noel could make out, nobody had been brave, or foolish, enough to resist Linda's demands – even the guy who lived directly across the street from them at number thirty-seven. Noel had seen him, a man in his early thirties, coming and going, often heading off towards the woods, presumably for walks. Noel had said hello on their first encounter and the neighbour, who always wore a blue baseball cap, had grunted in response. Yes, even Mr Unfriendly had strung up a few lights in the bushes at the front of his house.

Noel couldn't see him now, but everyone else appeared to be here. Linda's immediate neighbour had set up a stall from which she and her teenage children served hot chocolate and mulled wine. A group of children had formed a choir, singing an assortment of carols and seasonal pop songs. There must have been a hundred people here, some with dogs, all of them – the people, not the dogs – wrapped up in parkas and woolly hats and scarves.

'Nice night for it,' said a voice behind Noel, and both he and Dani turned to find themselves looking at a man they hadn't met before. He was around Linda and Alan's age, with thick hair that had turned almost completely white.

'I'm Tony,' he said, introducing himself. 'I live there.' He pointed at the house next door to Linda and Alan.

They told him their names. 'Number fourteen.' Tony was holding a cup of mulled wine, which he took a sip from. His eyes twinkled with mirth as he said, 'Did Linda drop off the instructions on what and what not to do?'

Dani replied: 'She did. Nothing that flashes. Nothing inappropriate like a Santa dropping his trousers. Absolutely no tinsel!'

'Tinsel is the greatest threat to civilization,' Tony said. 'The temptation to cover my entire house with it was so great.'

'Linda's very nice, though,' Noel said, feeling like he was being too negative about this woman who had been so welcoming to them.

'Oh yes. A lovely woman. Just, I think she forgets sometimes that we're not her students. You know, she's best mates with the governor of the prison too. Peas in a pod, they are. But yes, very nice.'

He lifted his cup in a toast, and Noel and Dani did the same with theirs. The mulled wine was delicious, with a hint of cinnamon. No spice mix-ups here.

'How long have you lived here?' Noel asked.

'I moved in last November.'

'And what do you do?'

'Local government,' Tony said. 'I was actually involved in getting planning permission for this whole development. If you ever want to put in an extension or build a replica of the Eiffel Tower in your back garden, I'm your man.'

'I'll remember that.'

'Here we go,' Tony said, nodding towards where Linda and Alan stood. Alan was a slight, bald man wearing a fleece and a slightly dazed expression. Noel craned his neck to see over the heads of the people in front of him, as Linda raised her hand to signify she was about to start.

'My husband, Alan, and I are thrilled to welcome you to this year's big switch-on! It's such a delight to see so many of you here.'

'Like a great herd of reindeer,' added Alan.

'Quite. We're so proud . . .'

'Or elves. Gathering around Santa's workshop.'

Linda took a step away from her husband. 'As I was saying, we are so proud of this lovely little community . . .' She went on, explaining how it was going to work. 'We're going to switch on our lights first, and then it would be wonderful if one person from each household could go back and turn theirs on, before rejoining us for as long as you like. Alan, dear husband, would you like to do the honours?'

Noel noticed now that Alan was clutching

a remote-control device which he held aloft as Linda started a countdown from ten, which the whole gathering joined in with.

'Let there be light!' Linda called, and Alan pressed the button. For a second, nothing happened, and then all the lights blinked on, illuminating the tree and the roof, the reindeer and the star. Everyone cheered, and Noel couldn't deny it – it looked beautiful. Perhaps the mulled wine had something to do with it, but a warm glow spread through him, a sense of belonging that he'd never known before, a ripple of joy that made him pull Dani against him, hoping she felt it too. This place, it really was perfect. They were going to be so happy here.

'Go go go!' Linda called, and people peeled away from the crowd, hurrying to their houses up and down the crescent. Noel went too. He'd taken yesterday off work to decorate, following Linda's guidelines. It was all plugged in to an external socket, which he switched on now. He had this fear that there might be a loose bulb, that even though he'd tested it yesterday, it wouldn't work, but he had nothing to worry about. All the lights he'd strung on the tree in their front garden lit up, along with the lettering he'd attached to the front of the house spelling out Peace and Goodwill.

Noel stood and watched similar displays appear on houses along the street, then hurried back to join Dani, who was still chatting with Tony. Linda and Alan were in their group too, as was, to Noel's surprise, the unfriendly neighbour who always wore a baseball cap.

'Have you met Justin?' Tony asked.

Justin was holding a cup of hot chocolate and had a smear of cream on his upper lip which he seemed unaware of. He nodded hello, but didn't smile.

'We haven't met,' Noel said, 'but I've seen you around.'

'Justin is a prison officer,' Tony said.

'Oh, interesting. At Franklin Grange?'

Justin's voice was thin, a little nasal. 'It's not that interesting.'

'Even with your famous prisoners?' Tony asked. He addressed Noel and Dani: 'Lucy Newton is locked up there.'

'Really?' Dani sounded shocked. 'I assumed she'd be in some maximum-security place. Broadmoor or somewhere.'

'Broadmoor is a psychiatric hospital,' Justin said. 'And it's for men only. Women go to Rampton, near Nottingham.'

'But isn't Lucy Newton a dangerous psycho-path?' Dani asked. 'Didn't she murder, like, twenty elderly people in that care home where she worked?'

'I can't comment. I'm not allowed to talk about individuals who are housed at Franklin Grange.' Justin paused. 'But it was eighteen people.'

'She murdered more people later, though, didn't she? Some woman who was helping her?'

He looked irritated. 'Like I said, I'm not allowed to talk about individual inmates. It wouldn't be ethical.'

'Quite right,' said Linda. 'It would be like asking me to talk about any of my Brookes High girls.'

'I'm lost,' Noel admitted. 'I've never heard of Lucy Newton.'

Dani was clearly shocked. 'I can't believe that. You've never heard of the Dark Angel?'

'You know I'm not interested in true crime.'

'This wasn't just true crime. This was *news*.' Dani wrapped her arms around herself, as if the men-tion of Lucy Newton had made her go cold. 'She worked in a nursing home in London, where she murdered eighteen of the residents and made it look like they'd died of natural causes. If I remember correctly, one of her neighbours found evidence in her flat and she was sent to prison, but then got out on appeal.'

'It was a technicality, I think,' Tony said.

'Yes, that's right. After she got out she tried to get revenge on her old neighbours, then went on the run. They eventually discovered that her literary agent had been helping her and they caught her again.'

'Wait.' Noel was confused. 'A literary agent? Was she a writer?'

'No. But after she was freed on appeal that first time, she published a memoir. *An Innocent Woman*, I think it was called. All about how misunderstood she was. But it turned out that she'd written another, secret version. One in which she confessed to everything. They used that to convict her of all the crimes.'

'I bet that memoir would be an interesting read,' Tony said. 'A glimpse into the mind of a psychopath.'

Dani hugged herself even more tightly. 'Terrifying. And she's in an open prison just a few miles from here?'

Justin took his baseball cap off for a moment, revealing a grade-two buzzcut, and said, 'You don't need to worry. It's called an open prison but it would still be extremely difficult to get out. In fact, we've never had a breakout. No one has even come close.'

At that moment, the children's mini choir started up again, singing 'Santa Baby'.

Dani pulled a face.

'Not a fan of this song?' Linda asked. She seemed pleased that the subject had moved on.

'It's not that. I just don't like it when kids sing about, well, subjects that should only be for adults. I know, I sound so prudish, but this song is too . . . sexy.' She laughed as she said it, but Noel knew she meant it. 'For children to sing, I mean.'

'I think it's more about wanting some chap to buy you loads of expensive presents,' Linda said.

'Even worse. And whenever I see women singing it they are always dressed in those ridiculous little sexy Santa outfits. You wouldn't catch me dead in one of those.'

Linda laughed. 'Poor Noel. That's all your Christmas dreams shattered.'

Noel was speechless. He was also aware that everyone was looking at him.

'Dani doesn't need to wear one of those outfits to look good,' he said. But while Linda laughed and Dani rolled her eyes, clearly embarrassed but still smiling, he noticed Justin staring at her. Like he was imagining her in a sexy outfit. Alan seemed interested too.

'I'm so pleased you two have moved into the neighbourhood,' Linda said. 'Like I told you before, it's lovely to have young, fresh blood here.'

'Now you sound like a serial killer,' said Alan, speaking for the first time. 'I bet that's the kind of thing Lucy Newton says to her victims.'

'Oh, don't be silly, Alan.'

She turned away, and Noel noticed the smile slip from Alan's face, to be replaced by a glare of resentment aimed at his wife's back. Alan's feelings had clearly been hurt.

Shortly afterwards, the group dispersed, and Noel and Dani headed home. When they reached their doorstep, she fished in her bag for her keys, and Noel found himself gazing at her, the new Christmas lights playing on her skin and hair. She looked like an angel.

'Why are you staring at me like that? You're not picturing me in one of those outfits, are you?'

'Um . . .'

She laughed. 'Such a typical bloke.'

'I can't help it.'

They went inside and Noel turned to close the door.

As he did so, he caught movement across the street, outside number thirty-seven. Someone, presumably Justin, was standing on the lawn in the shadows, the lights on the tree not bright enough to reveal his face. But Noel could sense it. He was watching them. And he was still watching them when Noel closed the door.

4

If you asked the average person if a psychopathic serial killer would be a fan of Christmas, they would almost certainly say, *Are you crazy?* Christmas is the season of goodwill to all men and women. A time for generosity and love, of families coming together and children's faces lighting up as they see what Santa has left beneath the tree. Nativity plays and open fires and *It's a Wonderful Life* on TV. A time when the Grinch learns his lesson and Bruce Willis reunites with his wife after fighting off a building full of baddies. Surely those were all things that would make a serial killer want to sharpen their axe and go on a spree.

Not Lucy Newton, though. She was a big fan of the festive season.

It was the perfect time to wreak havoc.

To make tears flow like a melting snowman.

Lucy knew that people always let their guards down in December. They were too busy focusing on their shopping lists, planning get-togethers and worrying about whether their mother-in-law was going to be a nightmare again. On top of that, everyone drank too much.

Back in her former life, before they caught her and locked her up, Lucy and her husband, Chris, had seen Christmas as a special hunting season. There had been this one time when this sappy couple who lived in the flat above them – Letitia and David – had gone on and on about how much they were looking forward to spending their first Christmas together in their new flat. They were having friends round for dinner and planning on cooking a huge feast. On Christmas morning, Chris had cut the power to their flat, as well as the gas supply, meaning they couldn't cook their turkey and their flat was bitterly cold. This was after she'd spent weeks intercepting all their parcels and sending them back to the retailers with 'not known at this address' on the labels.

Little things. But a fun appetizer for all the mayhem that followed.

She wasn't sure how much fun she was going to have in HMP Franklin Grange this Christmas, even though a lot of the women were excited about it, especially after yesterday, when the governor had announced at her weekly address that they were going to stage 'something special' on the twenty-fourth.

'A show for all the inmates,' she had said.

'Strippers!' one of the women had yelled out, which had drawn a huge roar of mirth and approval.

The governor, Patricia Jarrett, had waited for the fuss to die down, then said, 'We thought perhaps a Christmas-themed play . . .'

She had droned on for a while and Lucy had tuned out, thinking that on the day of the show she would probably plead sickness and stay in her cell – or room, as they called them here.

It was remarkable to some that Lucy, who was serving a whole life sentence for multiple murder, was now in an open prison. But she had been a model prisoner all the years she'd been inside: cooperative, helpful and charming to the officers and other staff. She was very good at pretending to be one of the herd; it was something she had practised her whole life. Normality was camouflage, and she wore it well.

But she had still been surprised when the governor of the place where she was banged up previously, a far harsher institution than this one, had told Lucy she had been chosen for an experimental programme. They were going to place several women with whole life sentences, women who had been found guilty of terrible crimes, in Franklin Grange. She had soon learned that this place wasn't really *open*. It still had a fence around it. Walls and gates and heavy doors. She couldn't just stroll out and vanish.

It was, though, compared to other prisons, a pleasant place to be detained. Lucy took on the job of looking after the hens, something she enjoyed far more than she'd anticipated. The inmates were able to move around the place relatively freely. The food was healthy, a lot of it grown in the grounds.

It was still a prison, though.

And Lucy was not born to be caged.

She was on her way back from the chicken enclosure, intending to spend some time alone in her room, when she heard quick footsteps behind her. It was Patricia, who prided herself on patrolling the corridors and communing with her 'ladies'.

'Ms Newton,' she called.

Lucy conjured up a pleasant smile. 'Mrs Jarrett.'

Patricia, who Lucy had some respect for – she might have been a control freak and a busybody, but she didn't put up with any BS – returned Lucy's smile. 'Come with me. I've got someone I'd like you to meet.'

Lucy tensed. The officials here were always forcing her to have long, pointless sessions with psychologists and criminologists. How they loved studying her, trying to figure her out, these so-called experts in deviant behaviour, most of whom – she was sure – were mainly interested in making a name for themselves by publishing papers about her. Or that was their aim, anyway. They would always leave frustrated, wondering how someone who seemed this average and placid could be so notorious.

She followed Patricia through a door into the wing of the prison where the library was located. So that was where they were headed. The library was a centrepiece of the rehabilitative ethos of Franklin Grange, a place where women who hadn't picked up a book since school discovered a love of reading, or even learned to read. Apart from the chicken enclosure, it was Lucy's favourite place in the prison. A quiet sanctuary, away from all the gossip and nonsense and chatter that made the inside of her head itch.

On the far side of the library, beside the shelves

that held the prison's collection of crime thrillers, a slim woman sat at a table with a pile of books in front of her, and an open notepad.

The woman, who appeared to be in her forties, with light brown hair and thick spectacles, got to her feet as the governor strode across the library with Lucy following.

'Lucy, this is Camilla Hart.'

You're sitting at my table, Lucy thought.

'She's got what I think will be a fun and extremely useful proposition for you. I'm going to leave you to it.'

Patricia exited, and a prison officer, a guy with short hair whose name Lucy couldn't remember, came in and hovered by the autobiography section while Camilla gestured for Lucy to take a seat opposite her. She was definitely some kind of psychologist, and she should be thankful that it would never be possible to prise Lucy's brain open. Anyone peering into the depths of Lucy's mind might just have time to let out a horrified scream before turning to stone.

'I expect you're wondering who I am and what this exciting proposition is,' Camilla said. 'Let me start by asking a question. Have you ever read any Charles Dickens?'

Lucy hadn't been expecting that. 'I think they made us read one at school. *Bleak House?*'

'And what did you think of it?'

All she could remember was that she hadn't read it. She had forced one of the class swots to write her essay about it. But what would a normal person say now? They'd make a joke. 'It was bleak.'

Camilla smiled politely then patted the pile of books beside her. She slid the top one off, hugging it against herself, the cover concealed. Lucy took in the titles on the spines of the other books, expecting them to be psychology books. But they were called things like *Unleashing the Bard Within* and *The Magic of Storytelling: A Stroll through the Forest of Dreams*.

'I'm a creative writing teacher,' Camilla said. There was the tiniest tremor in her voice, one that ordinary people would not be able to detect. She was nervous. That wasn't unusual – most people were when they met Lucy – but Camilla was also trying very hard to seem unthreatening and friendly.

Lucy could sense it. Camilla was here because she was fully bought-in to the Franklin Grange ethos. She was a do-gooder. Probably a vegetarian. The type who volunteered at a food bank and

sponsored mistreated donkeys. The very definition of a bleeding-heart liberal.

A good person.

Lucy's favourite kind of prey.

'Mrs Jarrett has told me that the women here
are going to be putting on a performance this
Christmas, and she thought it might be super for
that performance to be a play. Are you a fan of
the theatre, Lucy?'

'Not particularly,' she replied.

'Oh, well, that doesn't matter. I'm sure you like
movies.'

She didn't, really. The only films she liked were
home videos. The recordings she and her late husband Chris had made of their victims arguing or
getting upset because some other terrible misfortune had befallen them. Weeping with despair.
Cursing the day they were born. Those had been
thoroughly entertaining.

'We have a film club here, once a week,' Lucy
said, not answering the question directly. 'Last
week we watched *Elf*.' Infantile nonsense which,
predictably, the majority of the brain-dead inmates
here had lapped up.

Camilla wrinkled her nose. She probably only
liked foreign films. Ones with subtitles.

'Back to Dickens,' Camilla said brightly. 'Have you ever read or watched *A Christmas Carol?*'

Lucy had heard of it, of course. She wasn't ignorant. 'The one with Scrooge?'

'That's it. Mrs Jarrett and I want to create our own adaptation of Dickens's classic. We want to use the structure and themes of the book, and the main plot, but adapt it so it's more accessible to the audience we have in here.'

'I don't mean to be rude,' Lucy asked, wishing she could be far more rude. 'But what has this got to do with me?'

Camilla set her copy of *A Christmas Carol* face up on the table between them. The cover showed a crusty old Victorian man wearing a top hat and carrying a candle. A small boy stood beside him, leaning on a crutch.

'We want you to write this new version, Lucy. With my help, of course.'

'Me? But I don't know anything about plays or theatre.'

'You like books, though, don't you? Mrs Jarrett tells me you work here in the library. That you've been helping some of the residents learn to read.'

Residents! Lucy had to force herself not to scoff. It was true that she had volunteered to work here and that she had indeed taught several women to read. But she hadn't done it because she liked helping people or because she was a book-worm. She did it to win favour with Jarrett and the powers-that-be. To earn privileges, such as a room that she didn't have to share. Also, she genuinely liked it here, in this quiet room, and it gave her access to newspapers. They weren't allowed inter-net access and she liked to keep up with the news, such as the trial of an unnamed juvenile girl who had wreaked bloody mayhem recently. Lucy her-self was still regularly mentioned in the press, in articles about Women Who Kill or in pieces about how cushy life was at Franklin Grange.

'That's true,' she said, responding to Camilla. 'But I'm not a writer.'

'Oh, but you are. I've read your book, Lucy. *An Innocent Woman*. I looked it up, and you said that it wasn't ghostwritten?'

'It wasn't. I wrote every word.'

Camilla leaned forward, eyes glistening with earnestness. 'I could tell it was authentic. You have such a strong voice. A way with words. I was very impressed.'

Lucy felt herself warming to Camilla, as much as she could ever warm to anyone. Most of the reviews of *An Innocent Woman*, which had been published after Lucy was freed on appeal, before committing more crimes and ending up back inside, had called it 'self-aggrandizing'.

If only those critics had read the original version. The uncensored draft, in which she'd detailed all the things she'd really done. Extracts from it had been read out at her trial, but it had never been made available to the public or the press.

'With my guidance,' Camilla went on, 'I really think you could create an exciting and instructive version of *A Christmas Carol*. We are going to have to get a wriggle on, but I think doing it at speed will add a certain frisson and make it more real and, dare I say it, guerrilla.'

What on earth was this woman on about?

'We'll be writing, auditioning actors, rehearsing, and then, ultimately, directing the play, which will be performed here in front of the whole prison on Christmas Eve.'

'What if I say no?'

Now, for the first time, Camilla showed a steelier side. 'The governor is extremely keen for you to do this. Between me and you' – she leaned in conspiratorially – 'she thinks it might give her some insight into the closed book that is Lucy

Newton. It will definitely be frowned upon if you refuse.'

Lucy really didn't want to be sent to a different prison. Keeping Patricia on her side was a high priority. Perhaps if Lucy did a great job, which she undoubtedly would, the governor might let her get a cat, which she had been angling for ever since she'd got here.

'I get to choose who's in it?'

'With my input.'

'All right,' Lucy said, picking up the book and riffling through the pages. At least it was short. And she'd already had an idea about how to make this even more satisfying than any reward she might get for doing a job.

'I'm in,' she said.

She strolled back to her room, taking the book with her. When she got back, she found a Christmas card sitting on her bed. It was a piece of external post, the envelope slit open and the contents examined before it was delivered. Once, Lucy had found this violation of privacy irksome in the extreme, but she had got used to it. It wasn't like she ever received anything from people she actually knew. All her mail came from fans. People on the outside who thought they knew her. Who wanted to strike up a correspondence with a serial killer. Losers, in other words.

Back in the day, when she was first locked up, she received a constant stream of letters. These days, they were few and far between – and this was her first Christmas card of the year.

It was bound to be some nutcase seeking a thrill. She couldn't be bothered to open it so she tossed it aside and sat down with her new book.

5

The second parcel arrived on Monday, two days after the switch-on party.

It was Noel's work 'do' that evening, a tame affair at which he drank alcohol-free beer because he had to drive, and he arrived home at nine to find Dani in the living room with her best friend from work, Zoe. An empty bottle of wine stood on the coffee table.

'Have we got any more of that?' Noel asked. 'Oh, and hi, Zoe.'

'It's okay,' she deadpanned. 'I know I'm not as interesting as wine.'

'You're much more interesting,' Dani said. 'And yes, there's a bottle in the fridge.'

He went into the kitchen, and Dani and Zoe followed him in. Zoe did a similar job to Dani at the social media agency, creating content and wrangling influencers. Originally from London, she'd come to Shropshire, she had told Dani, 'for a man', deciding to stay after that relationship had finished. She had light red hair and when she wasn't at work she always seemed to be on the way to or from the gym. She was in sports gear now, long hair tied back in a ponytail.

Noel spotted the parcel on the counter. Like the first one, it was wrapped in red paper with a pattern of holly leaves, with a red ribbon around it, tied in a bow.

Noel approached it. 'What's this?'

'It was on the doorstep when I got home,' Dani said.

Noel read the attached label.

Hope you enjoyed the mince pies! This one's for the lady of the house. Secret Santa xx

'It's for you.'

'I know. That's what it says. But I didn't want to open it until you got home.'

Zoe smiled. 'Dani told me about the chilli mince pies. I think she wants you to be the taster. Although it feels too light to be food.'

He picked the parcel up. Zoe was right. It was about the same size as the box that had contained the pies but it barely weighed anything at all. He shook it and didn't feel anything rattle or move inside.

Mogwai had come into the kitchen and, like last

time, was staring at the parcel with narrowed eyes, like it was something she was deeply wary of.

'Maybe you've got a secret admirer,' Noel said.

'Oh God, don't say that.' She looked sick at the thought of it. 'There's a fine line between secret admirers and stalkers.'

Now Noel was alarmed. 'You don't think you've got a stalker, do you?'

Zoe looked from Dani to Noel then back again. 'That got dark quickly. I'll open it if neither of you wants to.'

'No. I'll do it.'

Tentatively, Noel unfastened the ribbon and tore away the paper, revealing another brown cardboard box with a lid.

'What is it?' Dani asked, as he removed the lid.

The item that filled the box was soft, which was why it hadn't made any noise when he'd shaken it. He lifted it out, holding it up for her to see.

'Oh, you're joking,' she said, as Zoe made a whistling noise.

It was a little red velvet dress, trimmed with white fake fur, a black belt across the centre with a buckle. There was a hat too, also red and trimmed with fur.

A sexy Santa outfit.

Dani took it from him and examined it, holding it at arm's length. 'What the hell?'

'I think maybe you do have a secret admirer,' Zoe said, with a shiver. 'So creepy.'

Noel took it back, checking the label. It was the right size for Dani. And it was well made so probably hadn't been cheap.

'It must be someone who was there the other night.'

'Please,' Dani said. 'Get rid of it.'

He opened the back door and took the box round the side of the house to the spot where the bins were kept, dropping it into the black wheelie bin.

'I'm hoping it was meant to be a joke,' Dani said when he returned. 'Like, haha, let's take the piss out of her.'

'Another prank?'

'Yeah. Or maybe it was someone thinking they'd be doing something nice for *you*.' She paused. 'It wasn't you who sent it, was it?'

'What?' Noel was shocked by the suggestion.

'Well, you told me you'd like to see me wearing one, and you were pretty tipsy on Saturday night.'

'I wasn't that drunk,' Noel protested.

'I think maybe I should go,' Zoe said. 'I don't want to be here if you're having a domestic.'

'It's fine,' Dani said. 'We're not. I believe him.'

'I should go anyway. Work tomorrow. Urgh, I don't know why they don't let us have the whole of December off.' She paused. 'I do think you're right, though, Dani. It's giving stalker vibes. Either that or it's someone with a very strange sense of humour.'

'Thanks for the reassurance.'

'Sorry. Just being real.' She turned to Noel. 'You need to keep an eye out. Look after her.'

Dani hugged her goodbye and she went out to her car, a little white Honda.

'So who was there when I was talking about it?' Dani asked, after Zoe had driven away.

'Linda, Alan, Tony and Justin.'

'Well, it really doesn't strike me as the kind of thing Linda would do . . .'

Noel wasn't listening properly. He was remembering what he'd seen as they'd come into the house on Saturday night: the figure standing outside number thirty-seven, watching them. He remembered, too, Justin's face when they'd been talking about the dresses. A lustful look.

'Are you listening to me?' Dani asked.

'What? Yes, I was just . . .'

'What is it?'

45

He hesitated. If he told Dani what he'd seen, would she march over to Justin's house and accuse him of sending the outfit? Would she make him, Noel, go over there and threaten to punch him? Noel didn't like throwing accusations at people. All he had seen was a look, followed by the feeling that Justin was staring at them as they went into their house. It wasn't enough. He made a decision: he wouldn't share his suspicions of the man at thirty-seven. Not yet.

'Hello?' Dani said.

Finally, Noel spoke. 'It could have been anyone. There was a whole group of people around us. Any of them could have been listening in.'

They were both silent for a minute. Dani went over to the front window and looked out. The street was so pretty, with all the shining white lights. So festive and welcoming. A man walked past on the other side of the road with a dog on a lead. Further up the street, a grocery delivery van pulled up. Nothing out of the ordinary.

'I hate this,' Dani said.

'I don't think it's a stalker, though,' Noel said, trying to reassure her. 'The pies were for both of us.'

He pulled her into a hug and held her. 'I'm sure

it's just some idiot thinking they're being funny. Hopefully this will be the last thing they send.'

He looked over her shoulder at the street, unsettled but also angry. When he found out who'd done this, who'd upset Dani, he would make sure they knew exactly what he thought of them.

But whoever it was, he wasn't going to let this moron ruin their Christmas.

6

Noel took another half-day on Wednesday so he could spend the afternoon wrapping presents, including those he'd bought for his nephew and niece. Over in the corner, beneath a tarpaulin, were all of Dani's presents, including a framed portrait of Mogwai that he'd commissioned from a local artist. He knew she would love it, more than the less personal stuff: the clothes and AirPods and perfume. They were planning to spend Christmas Day on their own here, see Dani's parents in Wolverhampton on Boxing Day then drive down to Kent to visit Noel's sister on the 27th.

At around four thirty, after remembering to open day 11 on his chocolate advent calendar – so what if he was a big kid? – he went outside to turn on the decorations.

Nothing happened.

He flicked the switch off, then on again, but the lights remained unresponsive. He sighed. Most of the neighbours had theirs on already, many of them on automatic timers, blinking to life as the sun set. After trying once more, he swore aloud.

'Everything all right?'

Linda's husband, Alan, was standing at the end of the drive, with several envelopes in his hand.

Noel called out his reply: 'The lights have stopped working.'

'Let me just post these cards and I'll take a look.'

Alan walked off then returned a few minutes later. He was wearing a black beanie over his bald head and the same fleece he'd worn at the switch-on.

'Hmm,' he said, removing his hat and scratching his scalp. He was standing so close that Noel could smell his warm, minty breath.

'Do you think it's a loose bulb?' Noel asked.

'Could be, although they were working fine yesterday, weren't they? Might be a problem with one of the fuses. You know, things tend to go wrong in new houses far more than old ones. When Linda suggested moving here from our old place in Shrewsbury I told her we'd spend half our lives fixing stuff. Or rather, muggins here would.' He gave Noel a conspiratorial eyebrow raise. *Women, eh?*

'We've been lucky so far.'

'The thing about luck is that it has a habit of running out.' He was crouched on the floor inspecting the external plug socket, cast in the glow of the security lights, which were working fine. 'Got something else we can plug in here to test it?'

Noel fetched a phone charger. It didn't work.

'It appears we have identified the problem.' Alan stood up, his knees making a cracking sound that made Noel wince. 'Mind if I take a look in your basement?'

'Of course. Thank you for helping.'

'Thank me when it's working, Noel.'

Noel showed Alan into the house and down the steps into the basement. It was a large space, perfect for storage, although Noel and Dani hadn't accumulated too much junk yet. It was dry and clean down here, without too many cobwebs. When Noel and Dani had been looking at houses he had remarked to her that this would make a great den for their future offspring.

He had left the children's presents on a trestle table. Alan eyed them. 'All set for Christmas, are you?'

'Mostly. These are presents for my niece and nephew down south.'

'I'm so out of touch I have no idea what kids are into these days. We don't have grandchildren yet, but when they do come I won't have a clue. I'll probably mess up by buying old-fashioned things like dolls and Rubik's cubes.' He chuckled.

Noel smiled. 'Rubik's cubes are popular again. And Barbie is back too.'

'Oh yes, of course. The movie.'

'Not that I would buy my niece a Barbie. And Dani wouldn't let it in the house.'

Alan had gone over to examine the fuse box, but he turned around. 'Because of her feminist beliefs?'

Noel laughed. 'Well, yeah, she is a feminist, but not because of that. Barbie is empowered these days. You should watch the film.'

'Not my cup of tea.' He turned back to the fuse box, speaking over his shoulder. 'So why wouldn't she let Barbie in the house then?'

Noel wished he hadn't said anything. Dani was a private person and he felt awkward sharing information about her. But Alan was waiting, and he was helping Noel out, so he felt like he should answer.

'She hates dolls. Has a fear of them. Actually, modern dolls like Barbie don't freak her out too much. It's the old ones she really hates. If she sees one in a shop window she has to cross the street.'

'Dolls. Huh. People are scared of all sorts of funny things, aren't they? Linda has a phobia of hamsters. Completely fine with mice and rats and gerbils. But hamsters. She says it's something to do with how they store their food.'

He turned his head and puffed out his cheeks.

Noel groped for something to say. He felt like he always did in the presence of men who had come to fix something in the house: clueless.

'A cup of tea would be lovely,' Alan said, filling the silence. 'Milk, no sugar. I'm sweet enough. First, can you show me where you keep your screwdrivers?'

Noel stood in the kitchen making the tea, relieved to have this reprieve. Dani would be home soon. He wondered if he would ever lose the thrill of anticipation at her return, that little knot in his belly that he still got when she walked through the door. Sometimes, he tried to imagine life without her. What would he do if she got sick or had an accident? Or left him? It was too awful to contemplate.

He had just finished making the tea, and was

about to take it down to Alan when his phone pinged to let him know he had a text. It was Dani.

I'm about to leave work but something horrible happened. Someone DM'd me on Instagram with a gross message.

The three dots appeared to last for ever and then disappeared.

What was going on? Noel had started to type out a message when a voice called up from the basement, 'That should do it,' and, a moment later, the lights came on outside.

Alan re-emerged, rubbing his hands together, and giving Noel a long, technical explanation of what had been wrong that Noel found it impossible to concentrate on. All he wanted to do was call Dani and find out more about the message.

'Thank you so much.'

Alan sipped his tea. 'No problem. Linda would go crazy if one of the houses went dark. So what do you think of the neighbourhood? Settling in well?'

'Yeah, totally.' He forced himself to concentrate. 'We love it here and everyone seems really welcoming.'

'Penny for them?' Alan said, after Noel paused for a long time.

'Huh? Oh. I . . . was thinking there's one person here who hasn't been very friendly.' His gaze went to the front window, to the house directly opposite.

Alan followed his gaze. 'Our prison officer friend? Oh, Justin's all right. He just needs to get laid, that's all.'

Noel had taken a sip of his tea and he spat it out, almost spraying Alan, who laughed.

'I suppose you're not allowed to say things like that any more. I should say, he could do with a girlfriend. If he had someone like your Dani, he'd be floating around the estate with a big grin on his face. As would I.' He leaned in. 'I wish I was young again. Although Linda and I have still got a bit of juice left in our batteries, if you catch my drift.' He winked.

Noel couldn't wait to recount this conversation to Dani. It might cheer her up.

Alan took a final sip of his tea. 'But yes. Justin. I know he can be grumpy, but he has a difficult job. You'd be miserable too if you spent all day in that place with those scary women.'

'Like Lucy Newton.'

'Exactly. You know, I read her memoir. I've got a copy at home if you'd like to borrow it.'

'I'm okay, thanks.'

55

'Suit yourself.'

Finally, Alan said that he had better get home. Noel opened the front door, looking across the road at Justin's house. The lights were off, and Noel assumed he must still be at work. As Alan walked up the road, hands in his pockets, Noel went back inside and called Dani.

'Hey,' she said. 'I'm in the car with Zoe. You're on speaker.'

'Hi, Noel,' Zoe said.

'Dani, are you okay? What was all this about a "gross" message?'

'It disappeared,' Dani said. There was a tremor in her voice. 'Almost as soon I'd read it and texted you, the message vanished. The account it came from disappeared too.'

'But what did it say?' he pressed.

'I can't remember exactly. Something like, "Have you tried your Sexy Santa outfit on yet?" What was the next bit, Zoe?'

Zoe spoke. 'I think it said, "Can't wait to see you in it. Just make sure you stand close to the window."'

'And then, "I'll be watching. Kiss *kiss*."'

Noel's insides turned cold. 'Did you get the name of the account?'

Dani sounded like she was on the brink of tears. 'It was a string of letters and numbers. Just nonsense. They must have been waiting till it showed that I'd read it, and then they deleted their account.'

'*Definite* stalker vibes, huh?' Zoe said.

'I'll be home in ten,' Dani said. 'We just need to stop and buy wine. See you in a bit.'

She hung up and Noel went into the kitchen, looking across the street at Justin's house.

Make sure you stand close to the window. I'll be watching.

He closed the blinds.

7

Ebeneezer Scrooge was a massive disappointment. When Lucy had started reading *A Christmas Carol* in her room, a few hours after meeting Camilla Hart, she had wondered if the book's anti-hero might be like her. One of her kind.

But it soon transpired Scrooge was soft. His cry-baby reaction when the Ghost of Christmas Present told him Tiny Tim was doomed had made Lucy groan. And the ending, when – spoiler alert – the old skinflint had sent boring Bob Cratchett and his millions of offspring a massive turkey and then put up his wages . . . well, it made Lucy throw the book at the wall in disgust. Old Scrooge was a changed man, full of chuckles and Christmas bonhomie. Not special. Not an apex predator. Just a tight old bastard who wouldn't give you the drippings off his nose, until a quartet of ghosts brought out the lovely, cuddly version of himself who'd been hiding inside all this time.

Sickening.

Still, it was easy to see why Patricia was so keen for the inmates to be fed this story in advance of their own sub-par Christmas dinner. It was that most terrible of things: a morality tale. And this place, Franklin Grange, was all about rehabilitation, about sending the women here back out into the world to live normal lives, the cycle of crime and punishment broken.

She was due to meet Camilla in the library that morning, to discuss how plays are structured. Did she really need that patronizing sap Camilla to teach her how to adapt Dickens? Lucy knew she was cleverer than her. Cleverer than anyone else in here. All she had to do was follow the structure of the original. Meeting the main characters. Being visited by the four ghosts: Scrooge's former partner, Marley, and then the ghosts of Christmas Past, Present and Yet To Come. And finally, the resolution, which, in the original, was when Scrooge saw the error of his ways and became Mr Generous.

She knew exactly what Patricia wanted. And she would give it to her. Up to a point.

Because Lucy had come up with a brilliant idea.

'I'm impressed,' Camilla said, an hour later, leaning back in her chair and removing her reading glasses. She lay them on the table and Lucy had to stop herself from throwing them on to the floor and stomping on them. The first time she'd been arrested, it was because she couldn't resist the urge to collect souvenirs, mostly reading glasses. She'd stored them in her flat along with a USB stick on which she'd collected the obituaries of her victims. A big mistake that had been used against her in court. She should have been happy with her memories. All she had done by keeping souvenirs was give the prosecution ammunition. The same with the secret version of her memoir. Okay, she hadn't been able to resist writing it, but why hadn't she deleted it straight away? Why had she felt the need to share it with her agent? She knew it was because she wanted to impress – and, in a sick way, scare – him. She had instructed him to read it then trash it. She should have known he'd keep a copy on his computer. Should have foreseen that one day someone would find it and use it to convict her. This time, there had been no technical cock-up on the part of the police. Her need to show off had led her here.

'You really get it,' Camilla was saying. 'The text, I mean.'

Lucy bristled. 'Did you think I'd be too stupid to understand it?'

'Oh, no, it's just . . . most of my students take longer to grasp the, um, meanings beneath the surface. Most people—'

'I'm not most people.'

Camilla flinched. 'No . . . no. Of course.'

It was rare for Lucy to let people in positions of authority see her death stare. This stare, so cold it could freeze the birds on the trees, was usually saved for her fellow prisoners. People who didn't matter.

It was risky, perhaps, to put Camilla on the receiving end of it. The teacher could go to the governor and tell her Lucy had . . . well, actually, what would she say? *Lucy gave me a funny look.*

She didn't think Camilla would be that pathetic. But it was pleasurable to see her shiver, to see her face go even paler and to hear the tremble in her voice as she stuttered, 'I'm – I'm really sorry, Lucy. I wasn't being condescending. I know how smart you are and I'm thrilled to see you engage with this so enthusiastically. I was worried the deadline might be too short, but I think, between us, we're going to absolutely *smash* this.'

She wanted to tell Camilla that there was only

one thing that was going to get smashed around here, but Lucy was aware that the prison officer, the same young guy who had been here the other day, was watching them.

So she smiled and said, 'It's okay, Camilla. I don't like people assuming I'm stupid, that's all.'

'Of course. I won't do it again.' Sweat gleamed on Camilla's brow. *I've still got it*, Lucy thought. *And you, Camilla Hart, should consider yourself extremely lucky. If we were to meet on the outside . . .*

She smiled her sweetest smile. 'I forgive you.'

There was a moment of silence, and then Camilla said, 'So, we should meet again tomorrow, work on the script. If you get going on it tonight, perhaps work on the opening act, and in the meantime I can work on act two . . .' She was babbling.

Lucy stopped her. 'No.'

'No?'

'I can write the whole thing myself. You keep telling me how talented I am. Show you have faith in me.'

'I'm not sure you'll have time.'

Lucy dropped her voice to a hiss. 'Are you doubting me?'

How quickly the power dynamic had shifted.

Anyone would think Lucy was holding a knife beneath the table. It was incredible what fear could do – to both the victim and the aggressor. For Lucy, it was intoxicating. A rush of endorphins; the thrill that had, for so many years, powered her and given her a reason to get up in the morning. Prison was so boring, like living in a time loop, every day the same.

She smelled the fear coming off Camilla. The *respect*. For the first time in years, Lucy felt like her bad old self.

'No,' Camilla said, her voice sandpapery, like there was no saliva in her mouth. 'I know you'll . . . do brilliantly.'

Lucy smiled and put some warmth into her voice. 'I have some suggestions for casting too. Scrooge should be played by Helen Bellingham.'

Camilla seemed shocked. 'Hell's Belle?'

'Her nickname has spread, I see.'

Helen Bellingham had been the matriarch of a south London crime family. Like Lucy, she was serving a whole life sentence for multiple murder, including her husband and various people who had crossed her, both male and female. She had been caught after attempting to dissolve her husband's body in acid, burning off the skin on her own left hand in the process, which had led to a hospital visit where, demented with pain, she confessed to the nurse what she'd done. She was another of Patricia's pet projects. If she could rehabilitate Hell's Belle, she could rehabilitate anyone.

'Are you sure?' Camilla asked. 'Isn't she . . . unpredictable?'

'She'll be perfect as Scrooge. You know, as well as being a gangster, she was a member of her local amateur dramatics society? She talks about it all the time. Acts like she could have been Helen Mirren if she'd put her mind to it. And if she's in, it will be easy to get all the other women on board.'

Camilla looked doubtful.

Lucy patted her hand. 'Don't worry. She's a pussycat really.'

A pussycat who'd claw your eyes out and use the sockets as a litter tray.

Lucy left the library glowing with satisfaction. Who would have predicted that being asked to help put on a stupid play could brighten up her Christmas as if she were out there in the world wreaking havoc?

She was almost at her room when she saw Andrea, the inmate who delivered the prisoners' mail. Andrea was a simple soul, harmless and diminutive, barely five feet tall. She might make a good Tiny Tim.

Lucy, who was six foot one, walked past her, nodding hello from up high, and was surprised to hear her say, 'Got a card for you.'

'Pardon?'

Andrea held out an envelope.

Another one? That was two this week.

'Go on, take it,' Andrea said. 'Nice to see you get some cards. You know . . . if you ever want to hang with me and the girls, you'd be welcome.' She was referring to the group of half-wits Andrea sat with at mealtimes. Half a dozen women whose combined IQs would barely scrape double figures.

'Go away, Andrea,' she said, taking the card into her room.

She sat on her bed and slid the new card out of its envelope. The front showed a house on an ordinary-looking street. There was snow on the roof and a tree lit up with fairy lights on the lawn. A parcel sitting on the house's front doorstep. She furrowed her brow. Had this card been hand-drawn? Was she looking at some amateur artist's efforts? It seemed to be. And what was that sitting on top of the tree, barely noticeable at first glance? She peered closer. It was a little magpie.

She opened the card to find a handwritten message inside:

Christmas comes but once a year
And when it does it brings . . .
Your humble servant, Secret Santa xx

Lucy was stunned. She turned the card over in her hands. The back was blank, no logo or text, which removed any doubts that this was hand-made. The writing was messy and child-like.

She read the message again, excited but confused. Because she knew how that rhyme ended – in her own version – but how could anyone else?

Christmas comes but once a year
And when it does it brings great fear.

It was a line from the unpublished first draft of her memoir. The one that no one had read – well, not apart from the police, who had used it to convict her, and her former agent, the idiot, who had kept a copy stored on his computer. But she knew it wouldn't be from him, and could hardly imagine a cop sending her this.

She scrutinized the picture on the front again. The ordinary-looking house. The magpie in the tree. That was what they had called Lucy at her first trial: a magpie. The prosecution had said she and her husband, Chris, were like 'those feathered fiends, renowned for destroying other birds' nests'.

Quickly, she found the card she had tossed aside the other day and ripped open the envelope.

She knew instantly it was from the same person. But this card was blank. Plain white. Strange.

She opened it to find a short message, written by hand. The same child-like, messy scrawl as the other card, like someone trying to disguise their writing.

Dear Lucy
The countdown to Christmas fun starts now
A merry old time awaits . . .

Again, it was signed 'Secret Santa'.

She looked from one card to the other. What could this mean? What Christmas fun?

She didn't understand it. But it made the

goosebumps stand up on her arms. A ripple of excitement that she hadn't felt for a long time.

Good things were about to happen.

Well, good for Lucy.

Bad for everyone else.

8

The third package arrived on the fifteenth. This time Noel and Dani found it together. They'd gone shopping at the big supermarket in Telford, getting all the things they had yet to buy for their first Christmas together, including a huge selection of cheese from a deli in town, which they intended to eat on Noel's birthday on the twenty-fourth in front of *Die Hard*. Sometimes the old Christmas traditions were the best.

'Oh no,' Dani said as they got out of the car and saw the parcel. There hadn't been any new messages since the one Dani had received the other day, and Noel hadn't seen Justin either. They had tried to put it out of their minds and hope that whoever it was, Justin or someone else, had got bored.

Noel picked the present up, little bubbles of dread popping in his stomach. It was in the same wrapping as before. This time, the label simply said *Love, Secret Santa xx*.

'Maybe we should chuck it straight in the bin,' Noel said.

They both regarded the parcel, and he knew they wouldn't do that. He needed to know what it contained.

Dani took it from him and weighed it in her hands. 'It's heavier this time. Definitely not an outfit. Or mince pies.'

She ripped the paper off, letting it fall on to the lawn. Inside was another cardboard box, identical to the others. Dani lifted the lid – and dropped the box. She recoiled, almost tripping over the doorstep as she took several steps backwards, a hand on her chest, covering her heart. In the glow of the security lights, she was ghost-white, breathing heavily.

Noel looked down. Inside the box was a doll. Not a slim, modern doll like a Barbie, but one of those old-fashioned porcelain dolls, with cupid's bow lips, big brown eyes and a mass of dark, curly hair. She – *it* – was dressed in a Santa suit. Not the kind of 'sexy' outfit Dani had been sent last time, but not too dissimilar. It was a plush red velvet cape, with a white fur trim, fastened at the front with a brooch that looked like a sprig of holly. It wore little gold boots and stared up at Noel with a beseeching expression.

He looked over at Dani. She had her back against the front door now, hands on her cheeks, unable to look at the thing in the box.

'Get it away from me,' she said.

He hesitated. His insides had frozen – because he knew he'd screwed up.

Dani was going to be furious.

'Noel. Get it out of my sight.'

He snatched it up, in its box, and put the lid back on it. He couldn't help but think it was like putting the lid on a coffin. To many people, this doll would be adorable. But he knew that, to Dani, it was worse than a spider, a snake, a severed head. And he knew, from one of the stories she'd told him when they'd first fallen for each other, why it freaked her out so much, triggering panic. Her trauma.

The terrible thing that had happened to her when she was a little girl.

9

'Be a good girl for Auntie Mary, okay?'

Dani's mum kissed her on the cheek, then left, heading back to her dad, who was waiting outside in the car. Dani, who was eight years old, was holding a little bag that contained her pyjamas, toothbrush and her paperback of *Matilda*, which she was reading for the tenth time. In her other hand she held her best friend, a cuddly rabbit called Buster.

'Why don't you go and put your things in your room?' Aunt Mary said. 'Have you had your tea? You have? What about pudding?'

Dani shook her head. It was a small fib. She *had* eaten pudding, but Mary always had cakes, ones she didn't get at home: Battenberg, and Dani's absolute favourite, lemon drizzle cake. It was one of the reasons why she wasn't bothered when her parents went out and left her here, being babysat. Tonight, her parents were going to her dad's work

Christmas party at a big hotel out in the countryside and were staying the night. They'd been talking about it excitedly for weeks. 'Our night of freedom!' her dad said when he didn't know Dani was listening. They were going to pick her up in the morning.

Upstairs, she deposited her stuff, placing Buster on her pillow, then went over to the bedroom window, watching her parents drive away up the lane, headlights disappearing as they turned the bend, leaving nothing but darkness in their wake. Aunt Mary lived in a cottage on the very outskirts of town, on the edge of farmland, some horses in the field that backed on to her garden. The nearest neighbour was a few minutes' walk away. Apparently, Aunt Mary had lived in this house her *whole* life. Eighty-something years! Dani couldn't comprehend it. She was like a character from one of Dani's Roald Dahl books. Eccentric, Dad called her. Never married, which Mum said was extremely sensible. No children of her own.

At least not real human ones.

When Dani returned to the living room she found a plate containing a big slice of lemon drizzle waiting for her, with a glass of milk beside it.

'You can't beat lemon drizzle, can you?' Mary

said, removing the plate, on which nothing remained but crumbs, a few minutes later. 'I can't eat it these days because it gets stuck in my dentures.'

Mary stood in front of her small Christmas tree, which was so laden with tinsel Dani thought it might fall over at any moment.

'I almost forgot,' Mary said. 'I have something to show you. A new addition to the family.'

'Oh.' Dani tried to sound enthusiastic.

'You're going to love her. She's a special one.'

Mary went off to the dining room, which was next to the living room. Dani's mum had told her that she needed to be kind to her aunt, to indulge her. 'I know it's a bit odd, but she loves them.'

'And they might be worth a fortune one day,' added Dad.

Dani sat back in her seat now and looked around at the objects Mum and Dad had been talking about: Aunt Mary's collection of dolls.

There were over a hundred of them, sitting on shelves on all four walls of this room. They weren't like the dollies Dani had played with when she was really little. They didn't cry real tears or say 'Mama' when you squeezed them. These dolls were most definitely not to be played with. They were made of porcelain, cool to the touch, with realistic-looking hair and wide eyes with long lashes. They were all as pale as the glass of milk Dani had just drunk, which didn't reflect the world Dani lived in, but Aunt Mary said that was because they were antiques. Made when Queen Victoria was on the throne.

'You should keep the most valuable ones in a cabinet,' Dad had suggested to Mary once. Mary was Dad's gran's sister. 'I can build you one if you like.'

Mary had reacted with horror. 'You mean put them behind glass? I couldn't do that. How would they breathe?'

Dad had laughed like Mary was telling a joke, but Dani knew she wasn't. When no one else but Dani was around, Mary would put on a variety of high voices, some posh, some with Cockney accents, as if they had escaped from the pages of *Oliver Twist*, and she would chat with her 'children'.

'Isn't it lovely that Dani has come to see us?' Mary would say.

One doll, a blonde in a frilly gown, would reply, 'Absolutely, Mummy Mary. I wish I were a real-life girl so we could play together on the garden swing.'

Then one of the Cockney dolls, a dark-haired

model, would say, 'But it's bloomin' brass monkeys out there. I'd rather be warming me cockles by the fire.'

Then a whole conversation would break out, a kind of puppet show, with Mary moving from shelf to shelf, thoroughly enjoying herself but – and this was the weird part – taking it all very seriously, like the dolls actually were talking. When Dani was five, she'd found it funny. Sometimes she would put on voices herself and get the dolls to say things. Once she had tried to take one of them off the shelf so she could play with it and she had dropped it, smashing it on the hard floor, and when Mary had seen the hole in the doll's face she had screamed and yelled at Dani. Later, after Dani had cried, Mary had apologized and made her promise not to tell.

Now Dani wasn't a baby any more and she didn't like the dolls. She didn't like the way they looked at her. Those staring eyes, following her around the room. They weren't cute like Buster. There was a smell of dust about them. Sometimes she had dreams in which they would come down from the shelves and march towards her, swarm her, with their stiff little arms and legs, those unblinking eyes, because she had something they didn't, something they wanted. She had breath and warmth and skin. She was a real-life girl. And in her nightmares, the dolls would try to steal that from her.

Aunt Mary came back into the room, carrying the doll wrapped in a cloth. She was a little out of breath, like she'd been running, and Dani noticed her wince as she set the parcel gently on the table, unpeeling the layers of cloth to reveal her newest 'child'.

'Isn't she pretty?' she said.

The doll was not pretty; not in Dani's eyes. She seemed even older than most of the others, with a spiderweb of cracks on her face. Her blue eyes were cold and dead, and the red outfit she was wearing smelled like the back of her aunt's wardrobe, where Dani used to enjoy hiding when she was little. Musty and tinged with chemicals.

'She's a special Christmas angel,' Mary said. 'Do you like her gown?'

Dani didn't. It was tatty. It stank.

'I'm going to the Christmas ball,' Mary said, putting on a soft, girlish voice. 'I'm going to dance with a handsome gentleman and have the time of my—'

Her face had screwed up with pain.

'Are you okay?' Dani asked.

'Yes, yes. Just a little bit of indigestion, I think.'

She wrapped the doll back in its cloth, to Dani's great relief. She had gone almost as pale as the doll. 'I should put little Christabel here back. You know, I thought you might like her as your present this year.'

'My Christmas present?' Dani hoped she didn't sound too horrified.

'Yes. She could sit on the shelf in your bedroom. Or she could live here, in your room, for when you come to stay.'

Dani was a polite girl. Naturally kind. But even she struggled to sound enthusiastic when she said, 'Yes, that would be . . . lovely.'

I don't want to come here any more, she thought. *Not with that thing in my room.*

'Oh, I do feel peculiar,' Mary said. 'Let's put you away, Christabel, and then I need to sit down.'

She went out into the hallway, carrying the doll. Dani didn't watch. She was trying to figure out if there was any way she could discourage Aunt Mary from giving her the doll. She thought perhaps—

A gasp came from outside the room, followed by the sound of something, someone, falling.

Dani hurried out, saying, 'Aunt Mary?'

The old woman was lying on her side at the foot of the stairs, her hand on her chest. Her eyes were wide open, like one of her dolls. She wasn't blinking.

'Aunt Mary?'

No response.

Dani backed away. And then she saw, beside her aunt, unwrapped from the cloth, staring up at her, the new doll. Christabel.

It killed her, she thought. *The doll. It killed her.*

Because she knew, from the way her aunt was lying so still, from the way she stared, the unnatural position of her limbs, that her aunt was dead.

10

Dani told Noel all this on one of the first nights they spent together, lying in his bed in the flat he shared with two friends. He listened, laughing at early parts of the tale, unaware of how dark it was going to get.

Dani was there all night, on her own. The phone – Mary only had a landline – was on a small table in the hallway. To reach it, or the front door, eight-year-old Dani would have had to step over her aunt's body. To go past the doll, as well.

Dani went into freeze mode, retreating into the living room, sitting in the armchair where she always sat. She wanted to go upstairs to fetch Buster, but the stairs were blocked by the body too. She was too terrified to go past the lifeless form. Too freaked out by the doll, Christabel, who she was convinced was cursed or innately evil. Staring at the doll in the darkness, she could have sworn she saw it move, rocking its plump plastic body towards the lifeless woman who had brought it here. She thought she could hear it whisper its disappointment; its demands. *The old woman has no breath left. Give me yours, little girl. Give me yours.*

Dani stayed in that chair all night, surrounded by the other dolls, all of them staring down at her. She thought she could hear them whispering to her too, telling her that she was to blame, that if she'd been nice about them this wouldn't have happened. They spoke to her in the voices Mary had used. Sometimes they fell silent and did nothing but stare, admonishing her. A few metres away, Aunt Mary's corpse grew colder and stiffer, Christabel beside her. The clock on the mantelpiece ticked. The Christmas tree glowed. And Dani sat there, too afraid to even go to the toilet or eat or drink.

When her parents arrived the next morning, at around ten, her dad forced the door down in response to her screams for help.

'What happened to her collection of dolls?' Noel asked.

'She left them to me. I didn't want them, of course. Didn't want them anywhere near me. My parents sold them at auction to a collector, so at least they all stayed together, and this person really appreciated them, apparently. At the time, I didn't care, though now I think it would have broken Aunt Mary's heart if she'd known I rejected them.'

She told him one more thing before closing the subject.

'Occasionally, some so-called friend thinks it would be hilarious to put a doll on my bed or to pop up and surprise me with one. I want you to know I do not have a sense of humour about it. If you ever think it would be a laugh to send me even a photo of a doll, our relationship will be over.'

He got it. It wasn't the kind of thing he would do anyway. But he got it.

Now he had witnessed first hand how phobic of dolls Dani really was. And he was almost certain he knew who was responsible.

'It was Alan,' he said, after they'd gone inside. Dani had scooped up Mogwai. She usually squirmed and demanded to be put down, but this evening she allowed herself to be held, as if realizing her important role in comforting her owner.

'What are you talking about?'

'The other day, I told you Alan helped me fix the outside lights?'

'Yes . . .'

'Well, when we were in the basement we started

talking about toys, because he saw the presents, and somehow we got on to dolls and . . .'

'You told him? Oh, Noel! Why?'

'I don't know. It was awkward and I was trying to keep the conversation flowing and I didn't think—'

She cut him off. 'Okay. It's done now. But what are you trying to say? You think Alan sent me this?'

'He's the only person on the estate who knows about your fear of dolls. It has to be him. He was there when you were talking about sexy Santa outfits too.' It must have been him who'd sent the message too.

'But why? Why would he want to torment us?'

'That's what I'm going to find out.'

He had taken his coat off as he came in. Now, he pulled it back on again.

'You're going to talk to him?'

'Yeah, of course I am. You think I'm just going to let this go? I'm going to find out what the hell he's playing at. If he thinks this is funny. Maybe he gets off on scaring young women. Maybe he's a psychopath. Whatever, I'm not letting anyone do this to my wife.'

He was talking himself into it, letting the heat spread through his veins, the burn of fury, the primal need to protect his nest. It helped him push aside the opposing urge: to avoid conflict, to keep the peace, to be polite. It also stopped him from even considering the other option: to call the police. They had no proof it was Alan. This was something he needed to deal with himself.

'Oh God,' Dani said. But she didn't try to stop him. 'I hate this. I thought this neighbourhood was going to be perfect for us.'

'It still is. Or it will be. We need to sort this out, that's all.'

He hesitated for one moment, then opened the front door and marched down the front path, Dani watching from the doorway.

On the way up the street, he rehearsed what he was going to say. He found ridiculous phrases like *I've got you bang to rights* and *Where do you get off on scaring women?* running through his head. It sickened him to think that Alan might have got some sick thrill from picturing Dani wearing the Santa outfit. He had allowed this man into his home. Shared something personal with him. This was supposed to be a respectable street, populated by respectable people. 'We're so proud of this lovely little community,' Linda had said at the switch-on ceremony. Did she know that her husband was at best a malicious prankster, at worst a predatory pervert? If not, she was about to find out.

By the time he reached Linda and Alan's front door Noel was so worked up that he was panting a little. He stood at the end of their driveway for a moment, getting his breath back. Their Christmas lights were on, inside and out, and one of their two cars, Linda's Audi, was parked on the drive. He rehearsed his opening line one more time – 'I want to have a word with you, *Secret Santa*' – then strode up to the front door and rang the bell.

They had one of those Ring doorbells, with a little camera, and Noel suddenly wished he had one too. It was easy to get security cameras these days. He should have installed one after they'd been sent the outfit and he made a mental note to order one as soon as he got home.

Nobody came to the door, so he rang the bell again. Was Alan in there, hiding from him? Oh, let him cower. Noel's blood got hotter and hotter. Maybe he *would* start a fight. He was younger, stronger. Maybe a punch on the nose would say more than a hundred angry words. Really get the message across.

'Everything all right?'

Noel turned. It was Tony, Alan and Linda's

next-door neighbour. The civil servant, with his full head of white hair. He was looking at Noel with his head tilted to the side, clearly concerned. Noel realized his fists were clenched by his side and he probably looked slightly deranged.

'I need to talk to Alan.'

'I think you'll have to come back. They've gone away. Went to stay with one of their kids, I think. Delivering presents.'

Something Alan knows all about, Noel thought.

'You okay, mate?' Tony asked. 'You look like a bull that's about to charge.'

Noel forced himself to exhale, wondering if steam was coming out of his nostrils.

'I'm fine.'

'You don't look fine. There's a big vein, right here.' He pointed at his own forehead. 'I'm a little worried it's going to explode all over me. Should I fetch my umbrella?'

Noel laughed, some of the anger ebbing away. As the red mist dissipated, he wondered what he'd been thinking. Had he really been on the verge of starting a fight?

'Do you know when they'll be back?' he asked, hoping he sounded calmer.

'In a couple of days, I think.'

'And when did they go?'

Tony narrowed his eyes at him. 'This morning, as far as I know.'

Noel and Dani had left for work at eight thirty. Had the doll been sitting there on the doorstep since shortly after that?

'Do you know what time?'

Tony cocked his head. 'What's with all the questions?'

Noel wanted to tell him. It would be good to have an ally, someone to share all this with. To sanity-check it. But if he told him he'd have to breach Dani's privacy again by sharing her doll phobia.

So instead, he said, 'It's nothing. Ignore me. I'll talk to him when he gets home.'

'I can give you his phone number if you like?'

'No. It's fine.' The adrenaline was leaving his body now, leaving him nauseous and in need of a sit down. A drink. 'Thanks for your help.'

He walked away, leaving Tony with a look of bemusement on his face. Noel was embarrassed, and unused to these feelings. Anger was not an emotion he was accustomed to. It was frightening how good it had felt.

As he passed number thirty-seven, Justin

appeared, dragging his wheelie bin and leaving it by the kerb. Of course: the bin men were due the next morning.

'Evening,' Justin said. As always, he was wearing his baseball cap. 'How's Dani?'

Noel did a double take. 'Why are you asking?'

'I saw you both when you got home. She looked upset.' He said this in a flat tone, his eyes straying to Noel and Dani's house, where Dani's silhouette could be seen in the front window. She was on the phone, presumably talking to Zoe.

'You were watching us?' Noel asked.

Justin frowned. 'What? I heard a commotion and looked out of my window.'

Noel immediately felt bad. It wasn't Justin who had been watching Dani. It was Alan.

'I'm sorry. I'm on edge, that's all. Ignore me.'

'Whatever,' Justin said. Then he turned and went back into his house without another word.

11

The bin men came the following morning, and Noel – who was about to leave for work – watched them tip the contents of the wheelie bin into the back of their truck, pleased that the doll was among the rubbish.

On his way off the estate, he drove past Alan and Linda's house. Half of him hoped they would arrive home that day; the other half would be happy if they didn't return for another twenty-four hours. This morning, feeling calmer, the conflict-avoidant part of his personality had re-asserted its dominance and he was pleased he hadn't found himself trading punches with Alan by their Christmas tree. He was still going to talk to him, though. Let Alan know he knew exactly what he'd done and demanding that he put a stop to it.

He spotted a familiar figure at the bus stop. It was Justin.

After thinking about it for a moment, he pulled over.

'Are you heading for work? Do you want a lift?'

Justin hesitated, obviously remembering their uncomfortable encounter the evening before. But he nodded and climbed in, explaining that his car had gone in for its annual service and that he wouldn't get it back till later.

'You can just drive me into town, if that's all right. I can get a cab from there.'

'It's fine. I can take you to work. I don't mind. A peace offering after being a twat last night.'

Franklin Grange was a little out of the way, but Noel's office was winding down for the holidays, nobody doing much work, and the boss wouldn't mind if he turned up late. This would be the perfect chance to get to know his neighbour a little better. He felt guilty for suspecting Justin of being 'Secret Santa' when he knew now it had to be Alan.

'So, yeah, I'm sorry about that,' he said as they drove away from the bus stop.

'It's no big deal. Was Dani all right, though?'

'Yeah, just . . . personal stuff. She's fine.'

'Cool.'

Justin really was a man of few words. Noel made several conversational gambits, which crashed and burned, as Justin responded monosyllabically. To drown out the awkward silence, he put the radio on. Mariah letting the world know she didn't want a lot for Christmas, which reminded Noel he still hadn't posted those presents. Too much other stuff on his mind. He would do it when he got home tonight – oh, except he and Dani were going to the cinema after work. Tomorrow then.

'What's it like working at the prison?' Noel asked as they drove through the village where Franklin Grange was based, unable to take the awkward silence that had fallen.

'It's fine.'

Noel pressed on.

'It's quite a liberal place, isn't it?'

'Yeah.'

Noel was trying to think of something else to say, tempted to change the topic to football or to ask Justin what TV shows he'd watched recently, when Justin shocked him by saying, 'They've got the women putting on a Christmas Eve show. *A Christmas Carol.* They've brought in some writing tutor to coach the prisoners and help them put it on. It's keeping them quiet, anyway. Distracted.'

When he had recovered from the shock of hearing Justin say so many words, Noel asked, 'Is Lucy Newton involved?'

'You know I'm not supposed to talk about her.'

'Sorry.'

The prison had come into view now. Noel had never been here before so this was the first time he'd seen it with his own eyes. A big grey modern building, surrounded by lawns and encircled by a fence. It looked more like a secondary school than a prison. As they got closer, Noel noticed a chicken enclosure in the grounds. After learning about the prison's most famous 'guest' the other night, Noel had searched for more details and discovered from a news story headlined FOWL JUSTICE that Lucy had volunteered to help look after the chickens before 'going back to her luxurious cell, complete with flatscreen TV'.

Weren't all TVs flatscreen these days? Noel wondered. But the details of Lucy's crimes, the elderly people she had murdered, the neighbours she and her husband had tormented, had sickened him. He knew that people could be cruel and vindictive and selfish. But to murder for fun? It was beyond his comprehension.

'She's helping to write it,' Justin said, surprising Noel as he pulled up outside the entrance. 'The Christmas play, I mean.'

'Who, Lucy?'

'Uh huh. Actually, I think she's doing it on her own. You know she wrote a book?'

'I think someone mentioned it the other night.'

'She's a clever woman. Creative. Misunderstood.'

Where was all this coming from? His voice had gone kind of . . . dreamy.

'You sound like you admire her,' Noel said.

'What? Oh no. God, no.' Justin's tone returned to normal. Flat. Expressionless. 'I just meant I'm not surprised they've got her writing this stupid play.'

He opened the car door and got out, saying, 'Cheers,' before walking away.

Noel watched him go, shaking his head. It really had sounded like he was a fan of Lucy Newton. But maybe that was common among people who worked with criminals. You started to see them as human, rather than the shadowy, mythical figures who are described as monsters in the press. A good thing, Noel supposed. He believed in rehabilitation too, in theory at least.

He took one last look at Franklin Grange, trying to imagine what it must be like to be locked up there. To know you were going to die a prisoner, with no hope of parole. He believed in second chances. In rehabilitation. Wasn't it cruel and pointless to keep these women behind bars for ever? He knew some people would describe him as soft. A bleeding heart. But he couldn't help but feel a twinge of sympathy for Lucy and others like her.

He still wouldn't want to meet her in a dark alley, though. And he definitely wouldn't want her living next door.

After work, Noel and Dani had dinner then went to the cinema. Every December, the cinema showed classic Christmas films, and tonight's had been one of the best: *Home Alone*.

On the drive back, Noel wound down the window to let some air into the car, even though it was frigid outside. Dani seemed better today.

'I talked to Zoe about what's been going on,' she said. 'She says I shouldn't let some creep who lives up the road ruin Christmas. She also said I should forgive you for blabbing about my phobia.'

'I've always liked Zoe.'

'Just don't do it again, okay?'

Glancing at her as she concentrated on driving, headlights illuminating the road immediately ahead, Noel experienced a surge of warmth and love, and a certainty that whatever life threw at them, they would be able to navigate it together. The road unseen, beyond the reach of the headlights. He could only imagine good things there for them. They were a unit. They were strong.

But as soon as they pulled on to their drive and Dani killed the engine Noel could sense something was wrong. He got out of the car. Everything looked normal, but the back of his neck tingled and there was a trickle of dread in his gut. There was no parcel on the doorstep. The Christmas lights were working, as were the security lights. Then he remembered the email he'd received when they were going into the cinema: the delivery driver had apparently left the camera he'd ordered on the front step, but there was no sign of it.

'What is it?' Dani asked, sensing his mood.

'I'm not sure.'

He went round to the side gate, to check if the box had been left there, by the bins. The gate was open – which was odd – but there was no sign of the package.

Feeling increasingly uneasy, he came back round to the front door and went through it.

The house was freezing. Dani came in after him and said, 'It feels like there's a window open.' They never left windows open, even in summer, because Mogwai was a house cat, not allowed outside.

Dani went into the kitchen and said, 'Oh. Oh no.'

The back door was wide open. Worse, its glass panel had been smashed. Noel looked down and saw fragments of glass around his feet, along with the key that they kept in the keyhole on the inside of this door. It was obvious what had happened: someone had smashed the glass, reached through and turned the key to let themselves in.

If Noel had felt cold on the outside of his body, it was nothing compared to how he now felt on the inside. He looked around the kitchen. It didn't appear that anything had been stolen or moved.

He moved towards the inside door, to check the living room. Nothing seemed to have been taken. But he had remembered something.

'We don't have insurance.'

She stared at him. 'Tell me you're joking.'

'We only have buildings insurance.' That had been a condition of the mortgage. But they had only been here a few weeks. It had been on Noel's list of tasks to sort out the contents insurance and he hadn't got round to it yet.

'Oh, Noel.'

'It's okay. So far we haven't come across anything missing.'

But surely the intruders wouldn't have left without taking anything? Noel felt like he was having an out-of-body experience. Someone, some stranger or strangers, had been inside their home. Their nest. He felt like he could sense them, smell them. He'd heard of burglars doing vile things in houses. Trashing them. Doing horrible things with toothbrushes.

Zombie-like, he left the living room and stood in the hallway.

The door to the basement was ajar.

Somewhere above him he could hear Dani calling Mogwai, panic in her voice, but as he forced himself to go down the steps he heard miaowing coming from below and he called up, 'She's here.'

He heard Dani's footsteps on the stairs above, running down to join him as he went into the basement and turned on the light. The cat was crouched in the corner, clearly scared. Seeing Dani, she ran across the room and Dani picked her up, cradling her like a baby, tears rolling down her cheeks. Noel was relieved too, of course he was, he loved that cat as much as Dani. But he was too busy staring at the empty space on the table where the wrapped presents had been. The gifts for his niece and nephew.

He went over to the tarpaulin in the corner, under which he'd been storing everything he'd bought Dani, including the framed painting of Mogwai. It was all gone.

They went back upstairs and called the police, then waited for them to arrive. Dani told Noel that nothing appeared to be missing from upstairs. There was no sign the burglars had been up there, but Noel still vowed to throw the toothbrushes away.

The police came, two of them – a man, PC Mayhew, and a woman, PC Degville – and they took a report which they said Noel and Dani would be able to use for insurance. Noel felt too embarrassed to correct them.

Mayhew went into the garden while they finished listing everything that had been taken to Degville.

'They probably came over the back fence,' she said. 'It's the worst time of year for it. People are out all the time and everyone has so much stuff in their houses just waiting to be taken. In this case, they appear to have been actively looking for presents. Brand-new stuff. I'm not going to lie to you. We recover very little of it.'

Mayhew came in from the garden, boots crunching on the glass that they hadn't swept up yet. Mogwai was locked in an upstairs room and they would need to clean up and put something over the hole in the door before she was allowed down.

'The back gate was open,' the male cop said. 'Also, I found this, lying on the lawn at the back of the garden. Something they dropped on the way out? One of your Christmas presents, perhaps?'

He held up the object and Dani shrank away from it, making a moaning noise.

Noel wondered if he was hallucinating. But no, it was real.

It was the doll.

12

'Anything for me this morning?'

Andrea, the diminutive postwoman, who had been distributing cards and letters up and down Lucy's corridor, shook her head. 'Not today. Expecting something?'

'That's none of your business, is it?' Lucy hoped her disappointment didn't show because it would be mortifying if Andrea or anyone else knew she had lain awake the last couple of nights wondering if her Secret Santa was going to send her anything else. She had the second card, with its illustration of the house and the magpie in the tree, beneath her pillow and she kept taking it out and touching it, reading the message and filling in the blanks in her head.

When it does it brings great fear.

Was someone really out there, creating fear? Someone who was inspired by Lucy's work? And if so, who could it be? A stranger, or someone she knew? She guessed it must be someone who had followed the court case, in which the prosecuting lawyer had detailed all the things she and her husband, Chris, had done to their neighbours. Hoax parcels and takeaway deliveries. Dead rats left on the doorstep. Loud music blasted at all hours. Little things designed to create unease and inconvenience, which had quickly escalated into a true campaign of terror, making the lives of the drippy loved-up couple upstairs an utter misery. It had been Lucy and Chris's mission; the way they got their kicks. For a while, it had been glorious.

Was this Secret Santa out there doing it for her? Paying tribute? Continuing her life's work?

She needed to know more.

'If anything arrives, I'll bring it straight to you,' Andrea said. Lucy had forgotten she was still there. 'I'm dead grateful you've put me in the play, by the way.'

'Camilla is in charge of that.'

'I know, but she told me you put me forward.'

In this gender-flipped version of the story, Andrea was going to play Bobbi Cratchett's wife while Tiny Tina, their unfortunate daughter, would be represented by a rag doll.

Andrea was looking at her, like she wanted to say something.

'What is it?' Lucy snapped. She was irritated now. Why was this woman, whose only purpose was to bring Lucy the message she craved, still here?

Andrea gestured for Lucy to bend down so she could whisper in her ear.

'I think you've got an admirer,' she said.

'What?' Was she referring to the card? Had she looked at it?

Lucy was about to yell at her for breaching her privacy when Andrea said, 'That guard. I've seen him giving you the eye.'

'Who are you talking about?'

'I mean, I don't blame him. You're a babe, and a lot of blokes like powerful women. Want to be dominated. I dated this guy once who wanted me to lock him in a cupboard and—'

Lucy cut her off. She really didn't want to hear about Andrea's kinky exes. 'Which officer?'

'Wotsisname.'

Lucy waited, fighting back the urge to grab Andrea by the throat.

'Jason, is it? No. Justin. He's a bit intense, quiet, but I wouldn't kick him out of bed. Mind you, after two years in here I wouldn't kick any—'

Again, Lucy interrupted her. 'Ridiculous,' she said.

Justin Graves was one of the junior officers. He'd only been here for six months, she thought. It had been him who had supervised her sessions with Camilla, standing over the other side of the library, watching them and making sure Lucy didn't stab the teacher with a pencil. She hadn't noticed him gazing at her, although she had been so focused on Camilla and the play, and distracted by the card she'd received from Santa, that she probably wouldn't have. To her he was as interesting as the paint on the walls.

She wouldn't blame him for lusting after her, though. She had met many men in the past who were like moths drawn to her deadly flame. Men with weird mummy issues, or who still lusted after the mean girl who had bullied them at school. Was Justin like that? And if he was, could she use it to her advantage? Get some special treatment?

She shook her head. This was stupid. Distracting. And it was almost certainly in Andrea's head.

Lucy dismissed the other woman with a wave of the hand, then headed towards the library for today's meeting with Camilla. She had the print-out of the play in her hand, the first half of it, which she had written over the last two days. Patricia had allowed her to have a laptop with a piece of scriptwriting software installed. Sadly, it wasn't connected to the internet, just the printer in the library. Apart from wonder about her Christmas cards, Lucy had done little else since she'd last seen Camilla. It had brought it all back: the joy of writing her memoir, especially the first draft, the one in which she'd told the truth about what she'd done.

Camilla tugged at her collar as Lucy approached, nervous after the way Lucy had acted the other day. That was good. It was important Camilla knew who was in charge here. But something strange: as she handed over the pages, she found she wanted Camilla's approval, her praise, even though she hated that her life had come to this: seeking validation from someone as pathetic as Camilla. It made Lucy, not prone to shame or self-loathing, despise the other woman even more.

She went over to the stacks, browsing the other books while she waited for Camilla to finish reading the pages. There, behind her, watching, was Justin Graves. Did he really have the hots for her? She turned her head to meet his eye and, yes, he blushed. Looked away. Did that mean Andrea was right? And was it the kind of crush he would be willing to do something about? It seemed unlikely, unless she worked on him.

Right now, she didn't have time to worry about that. She was focused on the play.

'This is amazing, Lucy.' Camilla beamed, holding up the slim sheaf of pages. 'I knew you were the right person for this job.'

'It's only half done.'

'I know, but you've produced this so quickly. And, honestly, I think it needs very little revision. I have a few notes, but nothing major. Well done. I love the way you've modernized it. Your Scrooge is so . . . human. I actually didn't think—'

Lucy waited, and watched as Camilla's cheeks turned pink. She was afraid of offending Lucy again. Of angering her.

'It's fine. You can say it.'

'Well. It's just . . . Patricia Jarrett told me you are not . . . a people person.'

Lucy knew exactly what Camilla was alluding to, in her cowardly way. She was trying to say that Patricia had told her Lucy was a psychopath, that she didn't experience emotions like ordinary people.

But what Camilla didn't understand was that Lucy had spent her whole life studying people so she knew how to act like them. How to camouflage herself. It was vital for someone like her if they wanted to exist in any kind of community, whether that was on the outside or in here. The sheep are always alert to the presence of wolves, so Lucy had been compelled to learn how to wear a fleece as a disguise. She knew what the fleece felt like. She understood lesser humans. So when she came to create the characters in her adaptation it had been a doddle.

The plot of her version of *A Christmas Carol* was simple. Emma Liza Scrooge was a hardened criminal who cared only about money. She had a couple of sidekicks who helped her run her criminal gang, extorting money from the poor. She lived alone in a big house where she enjoyed counting her cash but was too tight to put the central heating on. Scrooge had a partner-in-crime, Hayley Marley, who had recently died; a well-to-do niece called Freda; and an underling called Bobbi Cratchett who kept popping out babies, the latest of whom was called Tiny Tina. One change from the original was that Bobbi was a single mum with a load of baby fathers who wouldn't pay their child support, because Lucy knew a lot of the women in here would identify with that. They were always banging on about their feckless exes. Tiny Tina was a sickly child who needed medicine to manage her unspecified condition; medicine that wasn't available on the NHS.

'This is so powerful,' Camilla was saying, interrupting Lucy's thoughts. 'All the stuff with the ghost of Marley, the way he talks about his chains. The metaphor is going to be so relatable to the women in here. And it's really clever how instead of the afterlife you've made it so that Marley is forced to drag her chains with her in her life on the outside, after getting out of prison. Because, of course, Marley never got the chance to change her ways. She died a villain. Brilliant.' A pause. 'You know we won't be able to use real chains on stage, right?'

'Shame.'

Camilla laughed uncertainly. 'Yes. We'll have to rely on sound effects. Perhaps we could use paper chains? As it's Christmas?'

She went on like this for a while, praising Lucy's 'reimagining' of the Ghost of Christmas Past, a section of the play in which Scrooge revisited her childhood and got to see her great love, the man she'd lost because of her errant ways, happy with his new family.

'So we just have Christmas Present and Yet To Come to go.'

'I'll have them finished by the end of the week.'

Camilla's eyes shone with emotion as she said, 'Lucy, Patricia is going to be so happy. Do you want to talk through the ending? I think, don't worry too much about being a little blunt with the message.'

'Scrooge seeing the error of her ways. Dishing out gifts and vowing to go straight.'

'Yes. Obviously, we don't want it to be too cheesy. The audience need to feel the emotion of it. The moral we need to focus on is that it's never too late to change. That no matter what has gone wrong in the past, what mistakes you've made, you can redeem yourself. The future can be bright. Love can win out.'

'Do you really believe that?'

Camilla looked startled.

'I mean, can love win out for someone like me, someone who's not a "people person". Someone who has . . . done bad things.' She had dropped her voice. She never confessed to her crimes, but the temptation was great. She wanted to frighten Camilla. 'Someone who is serving a whole life sentence?'

To Lucy's great surprise, Camilla reached across and lay her hand on Lucy's arm. 'If I didn't believe everyone can change with the right opportunity and support, I wouldn't be here.'

No one ever touched Lucy without invitation. Anyone who tried got a smack in the teeth. It took all her willpower to stop herself from shoving the table at Camilla, knocking her off her chair. From taking one of those pencils and ramming it somewhere very painful. But she kept control of herself. Let Camilla's warm hand lay there on her arm. Out of the corner of her eye, she could see Justin, watching, curious – maybe jealous?

'I'll ensure that message comes across,' Lucy said, slowly withdrawing her arm from Camilla's reach. 'I promise it will give you and everyone here a proper festive glow.'

The same glow one might get watching a house burn down.

'Lovely.'

Lucy got up, keen to get back to her laptop. On her way out, she walked very close to Justin, so close she could smell him. Cheap deodorant masking his sweat. She didn't look at him. But she could feel his eyes on her as she left the library.

13

'I need you to get rid of it. I don't care where you take it. Just . . . *get rid of it.*'

It was the day after the burglary. The doll was outside in the garden. The police had left it on the counter in the kitchen, having explained to Dani and Noel that trying to extract fingerprints from it would be a waste of resources, but as soon as they'd gone, Dani had picked up the doll and flung it through the hole in the back door.

'I hope you can get all those presents replaced before the big day,' PC Degville had said before they left, telling Noel to make an inventory of everything that was missing.

How were they supposed to replace them? He had no money left. He had just enough in the bank to pay their bills, and he knew Dani was skint too. It had all gone on the house. And all the money he'd set aside to buy presents had been spent.

He wanted to punch himself. Why hadn't he got round to sorting out the insurance?

He was still asking himself that question over breakfast. In fact, in the middle of the night, unable to sleep, he'd gone online and taken out a policy – the very definition of closing the stable door after the horse has bolted. He knew they were lucky, really, that only presents had been taken. Mogwai was fine. Nothing with sentimental value was missing and the house hadn't been trashed.

For Dani, the worst thing about the burglary was the doll.

'You did put it in the bin, didn't you? And the bin men have come since then?'

'Yes. Yesterday morning.'

'And you saw the doll being emptied into the truck?'

He thought about it. 'No. I couldn't see what they were tipping in.'

'It's like . . . it's like the doll is my stalker. As if it came back on its own. Haunting me. Trying to scare me.'

There was a silence, which Noel eventually broke, saying, 'Dani, you know there's nothing supernatural going on here, right?'

'Of course I do.' She snapped at him, her eyes wild, and he wondered if she really did know that. If, somewhere inside, she believed that her aunt was haunting her, trying to give her the gift she had meant to give her the Christmas she died. Perhaps an irrational, child-like voice inside Dani was whispering and telling her that Mary's spirit was restless because Dani had refused her inheritance, selling the whole collection instead.

'Why are you looking at me like that?' Dani demanded.

'I'm worried about you. You don't need to snap at me like that. We're on the same side, Dani.'

'Oh, now you're making it all about you, like you always do.'

'That isn't fair. I was burgled too. It was actually all the stuff I'd bought that got stolen.'

'Yeah, *my* presents.' She stopped, and she covered her face with her palms. 'I'm sorry. It's so stressful, that's all. And even though they took the presents you bought for your family, it really feels like they're targeting me. The outfit, the doll, my presents being stolen.'

'We're in this together, Dani, whoever they might be targeting.' He paused. 'You know the burglary could have been done by a completely random person. In fact, I think it's more likely, don't you? There's no indication that this was the same culprit.'

'So why did they leave the doll?'

He spoke gently. 'It was probably already lying in the garden. The burglar probably didn't even see it. You know, I've been thinking, it could have been a fox.'

'You think a fox burgled our house?'

He ignored the sarcasm.

'I meant, it might have been a fox who got the doll out of the bin. I've had issues with foxes tearing open bin bags before.'

He was going to go on, but Dani put up a hand. 'I don't care right now. I just need that doll taken a long way away. Take it and hide it in the woods.'

'Are you joking?'

'I don't know. Take it to the tip, maybe. All that matters is that it's nowhere near me.'

They had both already decided not to go into work, calling in and explaining about the burglary. Both their managers were understanding.

Noel gave Dani a hug then went into the garden to fetch the doll, intending to take it to the tip. Its velvet clothes were damp where it had been lying on the grass. Could a fox really have dragged it out of the bin? He wasn't sure, but he did believe the parcels and the burglary were probably unrelated. That would explain how this burglary had happened while Alan was away. He still believed Alan, as the only person who knew about the doll, had to be guilty of being Secret Santa. They would probably never know who had broken into their house.

Going out through the side gate, Noel remembered something. The security cameras he'd ordered. The website said they'd been delivered and left on the doorstep. The burglars must have taken them too.

He reached the car, holding the doll upside down by its ankle, and realized he'd left his car keys in the house. He was about to go back in to fetch them when he caught sight of the woods at the far edge of the estate, beyond the fence. There was a picnic area about twenty minutes' walk from here, down by the lake, with a small car park and a couple of large dumpsters. Instead of driving to the tip, he could take the doll there. It would also give him a chance to get some air and clear his head. Think about what he was going to do next.

The entrance to the woods was through a gap in the fence just past the post box at the southern edge of the estate. As he neared the post box, he saw Tony coming towards him.

'I saw a police car outside your place last night,' he said. 'Everything all right?'

'We were burgled.'

'Oh, no. What happened? Did they get much? Do the police have any clue? I bet they don't – it's one of those crimes where they hardly ever catch anyone.'

Noel explained that the burglars had taken a load of Christmas presents. 'And yeah, I don't think the police are very optimistic.'

'Thank God for insurance, eh?'

Noel didn't respond.

'Oh, you're kidding?'

'We've only just moved in. I didn't get round to it. Massive schoolboy error.'

Tony patted Noel on the shoulder. 'That's rubbish. Wait till Linda hears. A burglary, here on Nightingale Crescent. She'll call an emergency meeting of the residents' association. Probably have people out patrolling.'

'That might not be a bad idea.'

Tony was about to walk away when he looked down at what Noel was holding. 'Taking your dolly for a walk?'

Noel laughed. Again, he was tempted to share everything. Unburden himself and explain why

Linda and her residents' association should be focusing on a particular resident she was married to. Instead, he said, 'It's a long story.'

He went through the gap in the woods and walked down the path beneath the bare-branched trees, pulling his coat more tightly around him as he went. The clouds were grey like steel and there was a bite in the air.

The weather must be putting off the dog-walkers, Noel thought, because there was no one around. The path was slick with dead leaves and the wind stung his nose and eyes. He was beginning to wish he'd driven to the tip. *Tony must think I'm mad, going into the woods with a doll.* He lifted it and found himself speaking to it. 'I'm sorry. Some little girl would probably love you.' Dani's aunt certainly would have.

He found that song from *Toy Story* 2 going through his head, 'When She Loved Me', which made him feel even worse. Perhaps he should abandon this. Clean the doll up and take it to a charity shop. It was probably worth a few quid; he might be able to sell it on eBay. But he was half-way along the path now, and such was Dani's fear of this doll, he felt he didn't have a choice. Get rid of it so Dani would never have to see it again.

Then, when Alan got home, confront him about the presents they'd been sent, although his priority after he'd dumped the doll was to figure out how he was going to replace the missing presents. Dani had, of course, told him not to worry. She didn't need anything. But it would be terrible if she had nothing to open on the twenty-fifth, especially as the presents she'd bought him were at her office and therefore safe. He also knew his sister would be understanding, but he still wanted something to take with him when he visited on 27th, even if it was just a token.

'I don't think my niece would like you,' he said to the doll – and at the same time, he heard something snap behind him.

He turned around. He couldn't see anything, or anyone, and he couldn't hear footsteps, but he had the creepy sensation that someone was there. The hair on the back of his neck tingled, his body – his primal self – telling him that danger was close by.

'Hello?' he said.

Nothing.

He walked on, even colder now, goosebumps rippling beneath the sleeves of his sweater. Again, he thought he heard someone behind him. A scuffling noise, like feet on wet leaves. He felt the sensation of eyes on his back. But when he turned and peered along the path, he couldn't see anyone. There didn't appear to be anyone in the trees either.

You're being paranoid, he told himself. *You're unsettled because of the parcels and the burglary. That chill on the nape of your neck is nothing but the wind. The noises you can hear are animals or birds.*

He walked faster, his hand tight around the doll's leg. He was almost at the picnic area now, but the panic was getting worse. He was certain he was being followed and that the person following him was dangerous. Meant him harm. He felt like he was going crazy, unable to keep these dark thoughts from swirling around his mind or to repel the icy fist of dread that squeezed his stomach. He found himself breaking into a jog, and it was probably the echo of his own steps, or his imagination going wild, but it sounded like someone was chasing him, a person with a knife or bat, the very person who had sent him and Dani those presents, a psychopath who wanted to scare them and hurt them.

Or maybe it's a ghost, said the most irrational voice yet. *Come to get its doll back. The ghost of Aunt Mary.*

By the time he reached the picnic area, he was

panting and wondering if this was what a panic attack felt like. He put the doll on a trestle table and bent over, hands gripping his legs just above the knee. He sucked in deep breaths and forced himself to look back up the path. There was nobody there.

He went over to the dumpster, lifted the lid and dropped the doll inside. It thudded against the bottom.

Then he walked briskly back along the path towards home. It was his imagination, he was certain.

But all the way home he was sure he was being watched.

14

It was exactly one week till Christmas – 'seven more sleeps', as everyone kept saying on social media – and Noel had spent the last twenty-four hours in a state of semi-paralysis, unable to function properly, as if he was coming down with a virus that sapped him of all his energy. Dani was the same. All she wanted to do was sit on the sofa in her onesie and watch comfort TV, working her way through all the cheesy Christmas films on Netflix with Mogwai curled up on her lap. Noel kept having to fight the urge to clean the house, even though it was already immaculate, to remove the taint the intruder had left behind. He was irritable, and the more he told himself he wouldn't let the break-in ruin Christmas, the more pressure he put on himself. At least his sister had told him not to worry about replacing the presents for the kids. They would get something and put Noel's name on it. There hadn't been any more unpleasant parcels delivered either.

The front doorbell rang.

'Oh,' he said, opening the door to find himself face to face with Linda. 'It's you.'

He hadn't been round to confront Alan yet. He'd found that, in the wake of the burglary, the weird pranks played by their neighbour didn't feel as important. He would talk to him when he saw him, but he wasn't going to march up to Alan's house and demand to know what he had been playing at.

'Noel,' Linda said. 'How are you doing?' Her voice dripped with sympathy.

'You heard about the burglary?'

'Of course. The whole street knows about it. Can I come in?'

She didn't give Noel the chance to protest. She walked past him and into the living room, where Dani lay on the sofa, still in her onesie, with the cat at her feet and a tub of Quality Street on her belly.

As Noel hurried into the room, Dani scrambled into a sitting position, Mogwai shooting under a chair and the tub of chocolates falling to the floor.

'Everything all right?' Dani asked.

Linda said, 'Why don't you take a seat next to Dani, Noel?'

Noel and Dani exchanged a 'what now?' look, but Noel did what Linda asked. Linda perched on the armchair opposite and Dani hit pause on the remote, Jude Law and Cameron Diaz frozen in a kiss on the screen.

'I love this movie,' Linda said. 'You know, my husband, Alan, used to look quite a lot like Jude Law.'

'I . . . can see it,' said Dani.

Linda sighed. 'You two youngsters have been through the wars, haven't you?'

Did she know about the parcels? Had Alan taken a break from being a Jude Law lookalike to confess everything?

'The burglary, I mean. Dreadful. There are a lot of security cameras on the street but none that covers the back of this row of houses. I've spoken to the rest of the RA about getting some installed back there and . . .'

Noel had stopped listening. Of course, a lot of their neighbours had security cameras! Why hadn't he thought of that?

'The burglar came to the front of the house too,' Dani said, interrupting his thoughts. 'They stole a box off the doorstep.'

'Which actually contained a security camera,' Noel added.

'How ironic.'

'Does Justin have security cameras?' Noel asked. His house was directly opposite.

'Yes, but Alan has already spoken to him. They're only triggered when someone goes on to his property. Most of the cameras on the street are like that. But listen. That's not the main reason I came here. I brought you something.'

She took a fat envelope out of her pocket and handed it to Noel.

'What's this?'

'The residents' association had a little whip-round. A collection. There's about £500 in there. Hopefully it will go some way to replacing what you lost. All the presents that were stolen.'

Noel was stunned. 'Oh my God. We can't accept this.' He tried to hand it back, but she pushed it back at him.

'Of course you can. This is a community, Noel. I'd like to think if misfortune befell any of us, the rest of the neighbours would help. And it's Christmas. If you can't do a neighbour a good turn at Christmas, well, what kind of Scrooge does that make you – as I pointed out to the people who grumbled about how you should have taken out insurance?'

Noel was so shocked by the generosity of his

neighbours that he didn't even feel the dig. 'Thank you. This is amazing, isn't it, Dani?'

She had tears running down her cheeks. 'I don't know what to say, Linda. To know that people care, it's . . .' She broke off, choked by emotion.

Linda said, 'Come here, you silly thing,' and pulled Dani into a hug, like a mother comforting her daughter. Afterwards, Dani found some tissues and wiped her eyes and blew her nose, laughing with embarrassment.

'It's all going to be okay,' Linda said. 'We won't allow anyone on Nightingale Crescent to have a lousy Christmas.'

As soon as she had gone, Dani said, 'I don't know how to feel. This is so lovely.'

'I know. I can't believe it.'

'But . . .'

Noel waited.

'It also makes me feel incredibly awkward. Because what if it *is* Alan who sent the doll and the other stuff?'

'He was the only person who knew about the doll.'

'Yes, I know but . . .' Dani raked her cheeks with her fingernails. 'Urgh, it's so difficult. We have no proof it was him.'

'Who else could it have been? Have you told anyone else about your phobia?'

She shook her head. 'I don't think so. Certainly no one around here. It's so difficult knowing what to do. Maybe we should keep quiet about it. See if anything else happens. I just don't want to risk causing any upset with Linda. Not until we're absolutely sure it was him.'

Noel went into the kitchen to get a drink. Pouring himself a glass of wine, a thought popped into his head.

He returned to the living room. 'I've got an idea,' he said.

15

Lucy and Camilla sat together in the hall, the communal space that was used for their weekly movie night, addresses by the governor and, tomorrow, the performance of *A Christmas Carol* that everyone in Franklin Grange, starved of excitement, was genuinely looking forward to.

The script was finished, the cast was confirmed and everything was set. Right now, the final rehearsal was taking place. On the stage, the female Scrooge, played with hammy relish by the famous Hell's Belle, was doing exactly what her male counterpart did in the original: making amends for her wrongdoing, going around being nice to everyone, surprising Bobbi Cratchett with her generosity and sudden seasonal spirit. The terrible fate that the Ghost of Christmas Yet To Come had shown Scrooge had been avoided. She, the gang boss and hardened criminal in this version, had vowed to try harder, to give up her life of crime, to ensure she didn't reoffend and end up back in prison.

Subtle it was not. But Lucy was strangely proud of it. Of course, she had always known it would be excellent. She was a genius, after all. But seeing the women perform it and take their bows at the end, Lucy found herself entranced and surprised. This was *her* work.

It was almost a shame she was planning to sabotage it.

'Brava! Brava!'

Her thoughts were rudely interrupted by Patricia approaching from the rear of the hall, clapping like she was trying to kill a giant mosquito.

Patricia reached the front of the hall and continued applauding the cast until they left the stage. Then she turned to Camilla, who had got to her feet, and Lucy, who remained seated.

'I knew you'd pull it off,' she said. 'Lucy, this is marvellous. The two of you have really exceeded my expectations.'

Lucy waited for Camilla to say, *It was all Lucy*. Instead, the glory-seeking tart said, 'Thanks, Mrs Jarrett.'

'I've told you a hundred times, call me Patricia. Lucy, you must be so proud.'

'Oh, I am, Mrs Jarrett. Although I couldn't have done it without Camilla.'

Again, she waited for the teacher to give Lucy the credit. She didn't.

'Who knew that Hell's B— I mean, Helen, would be such a good actress. Andrea is rather impressive too. Seems delivering mail isn't her only skill. The women are going to love it.' Patricia glowed with self-regard, because of course this was all her idea. 'We're going to have a proper party. Mince pies, non-alcoholic punch, and this play to top it all off. A reward for everyone's good behaviour this year.'

'You know they'd prefer a stripper,' Lucy said, which made Patricia guffaw.

'Maybe next Christmas.'

Camilla and Patricia went over into the corner for a chat, leaving Lucy on her own.

She felt eyes on her, and glanced up to see Justin, the guard, gazing in her direction. She waggled her fingers at him and he quickly looked away, the skin on his neck flushing pink.

So Andrea had been right. Justin had the hots for her.

Interesting.

Justin was standing by the exit, so she needed to pass him to get back to her room. As she went by, she 'accidentally' stumbled – the old tricks were the best – and fell into him, compelling him to catch her. As he caught her arm she heard his sharp intake of breath and then their faces were very close together. His pupils were dilated, his breathing heavy and she could smell a sharp, mannish odour of sweat and excitement.

She gripped his forearm before he could let go, holding it in place and looking right into his eyes. 'What did you think of my play?' She spoke in her most seductive voice.

'I . . . it . . .'

The poor lamb couldn't get the words out.

Lucy let go and left the hall, leaving him breathing heavily behind her. On her way back to her room she saw Hell's Belle, walking in the same direction.

Lucy hurried to catch her, calling, 'Helen.'

Hell's Belle stopped and waited.

'You were great,' Lucy said. 'Born to tread the boards.'

Helen grinned. She was shorter than Lucy, built like a human XL bully. She spent a lot of time in the gym here, lifting weights and doing squats, and she had also taken up yoga, which, she said, helped to take the edge off her inner rage. But only the edge – because Helen had a volcano inside her, an active volcano. She was always ready to blow.

'Life is theatre,' Helen said. 'You know I could have been as famous as my namesake.'

'Helen Golay?'

'Who the hell is that? I was talking about Helen Mirren.'

Helen Golay was a murderous pensioner known, along with her partner in crime, as the Black Widow. They had killed a couple of guys for their life insurance. Lucy greatly admired them.

Lucy knew that Hell's Belle found Franklin Grange boring. The other women here were too soft, too vanilla, and she would be happier in a regular prison where she could control her own gang of deviants. She had already tried to get transferred a couple of times, once by throwing a pan full of boiling water over a fellow inmate, and another time by telling Patricia she was 'a fugly slut', quoting her favourite film, *Mean Girls*. But Patricia refused to transfer her. Helen, along with Lucy, was one of her pet projects. If she could tame Hell's Belle and turn her into a model prisoner, she could tame anyone.

Helen would have to do something pretty extreme to get the transfer she craved.

Something in full view of the whole prison.

Which was where Lucy and *A Christmas Carol* came in.

'Have you learned your alternative script?' Lucy asked in a quiet voice, even though there was no one else around.

Helen chuckled. 'I have indeed. This is gonna be so much fun. It's kind of a shame we can't do two performances. One proper, to show everyone how good your script is, and how brilliant I am at acting, and then the one that's going to cause mayhem.'

'I can't wait to see Patricia's face.'

'Me too. If she doesn't transfer me after this, I think I'll have to kill her.' Lucy could tell she wasn't joking. She patted Lucy's shoulder. 'And don't worry. I know you like your cushy life in here. Your chickens and your comforts. I'll tell everyone it was all my idea and that you had nothing to do with it.'

'Thank you, Helen.'

Lucy continued on her way to her room, thinking about what Helen had said. Did she really like her 'cushy' life in this open prison? Like Hell's Belle, she was bored, but being here was so much better than being in one of the rough places where they'd first locked her up. Lucy was an expert in *psychological* torture and manipulation. She wasn't a fighter and had always used others to do the physical, dirty work for her, like her late husband, Chris, and the other helpers she'd had. She didn't want to be in a psychiatric unit either, with doctors poking at her brain and medication to dull her wits and spirit. This place was the best option for her.

But it was still a prison. Her room was still a cell. She would never walk out of here, and while most of the time she was able to stop herself from thinking about that, sometimes it hit her, and it hit her hard. She might be here for another forty years.

Or rather, her body might live for another forty years. But her essence, her dark heart, would wither and die long before that.

By the time she reached her room, she was in a gloomy mood – until she saw what was lying on her bed.

Another card.

She snatched it up. It had already been opened and checked by prison staff, so she knew it wouldn't contain anything explicit; any message would be in code.

This card wasn't hand-illustrated like the last one. Nor was it blank. This card was shop-bought, glossy with a picture of a snow globe on the front. Inside the globe was a house, not dissimilar to the one on the second card. But there was something inside, and when she opened it that something fell out, dropping at her feet.

She picked it up. It was an A3 sheet of thick, cream-coloured paper. She unfolded it and found herself looking at a painting of a cat. It had long fur and big tufts on its ears. A Maine Coon, Lucy thought. She'd always wanted one. But who had painted this? It wasn't a copy or a print: this was an original painting, created with watercolours. There was a signature at the bottom, but it was nothing more than a squiggle and was unreadable. There was a title beside the signature, though: 'Mogwai'. And, next to that, the artist had written, *For Dani. Happy Christmas, love Noel xx*

She lay the painting on her bed, feeling a little annoyed it had been folded, because it would look good on her wall, even with someone else's names written on it. For Dani . . . love Noel. Who were these people?

She opened the card and read the message inside.

'Take someone's life, and shake it up.'
This is my gift to you. But I'm getting bored now.
Happy Christmas, love Secret Santa aka

Beneath that there was a little doodle. Lucy squinted at it. A magpie.

Take someone's life and shake it up was another line from Lucy's book – the unpublished, fully confessional draft of her memoir. A line from a paragraph about how she got her kicks. But how on earth had this person, this Secret Santa, read her book? Who were they?

She tried to remember the rest of the paragraph that she'd written. What was it? *Take someone's life, and shake it up. Make them think they're going crazy. Scare them, wreck their plans, shake and shake again. Then, when you're bored of that, utterly destroy them.*

Yep, that was it. Words Lucy had once lived by. And someone was clearly out there, taking inspiration, paying tribute. She hoped Secret Santa wasn't planning to harm the cat, although if they'd read her book they would know not to. But Dani and Noel . . . well, unless Lucy was being stupid, they were clearly the targets of Secret Santa's campaign.

If she was reading these messages, these

allusions to her book, correctly, she knew exactly what Santa was up to.

Secret Santa had said they were getting bored now.

And that meant, if they were following Lucy's blueprint, they were about to go in for the kill.

16

Monday night, 23 December, and the party was just getting started. Noel had made a playlist, combining Christmas classics, current bangers and a load of songs that he thought would appeal to the older residents of the street, the kind of songs that fill the floor at weddings: 'Come On, Eileen', 'I Wanna Dance with Somebody'. Mogwai was safely secured upstairs in the bedroom, and Dani, who looked so hot in her little black dress that Noel couldn't stop staring at her, was greeting guests at the front door.

'I thought I was going to have to spend the evening on my own watching Ant and Dec,' said Tony, coming into the house and handing Noel a bottle of red wine. 'But you know you didn't have to do this. You're probably spending all the money we raised in the whip-round.'

'That's why we made it a bring-your-own-bottle party. We've hardly spent a penny.'

'Glad to hear it.'

Noel left Tony chatting with another couple who lived further down the street, then heard Dani call his name. Linda and Alan had arrived, bringing with them several bottles of champagne, chilled and streaked with condensation.

'Happy Christmas,' Alan said, following Noel into the kitchen. Noel opened one of the bottles and poured Alan a glass. Linda had gone into the living room, where around a dozen neighbours were already gathered, filling the whole space and making Noel realize how small their house was. There were more people in the dining room and even a few in the garden, smoking or vaping.

This party was a genuine way of saying thank you to their neighbours for their kindness and generosity, but it was also designed to allow them to get a better look at Alan. To see how he acted around them. They had invited a few friends and colleagues too.

After touring the house to check in with everyone and to see who was here, Noel went back to the kitchen, where Tony and Justin were chatting. Something about the local council's plans to redevelop a brownfield site a few miles away, turning it into a leisure park. Tony was on the committee that was responsible for overseeing the project.

'It needs cleaning up, though,' Tony said. 'Dirty work. Which is why we're thinking of enlisting help from the prison. Getting those women working.'

Noel was shocked. 'Does that kind of thing still go on?' He had visions from movies he'd seen. Prisoners in orange jumpsuits, overseen by stern guards with guns.

'Oh yes. It's all part of their rehabilitation. Getting them to do good work in the community.'

'Maybe Lucy Newton will be part of it,' Noel said, addressing Justin. 'When she's not adapting *A Christmas Carol.*'

'Oh yes, I heard about that,' Tony said, before Justin, who was, of course, wearing his baseball cap, could answer. 'The prison has actually invited a load of local dignitaries and business types to go along to watch.'

'Really? Are you going?'

'I'm not sure I fancy it. I imagine it will be dreadful.'

'I've heard it's actually pretty good,' Justin said, prickling visibly, as if Tony had offended him. 'The writing teacher they've got in has been raving about it, saying how talented Lucy is.' Noel noticed that Justin sounded a little tipsy.

'I thought you weren't allowed to talk about her?' said Tony, winking at Noel.

'I'm not. But if I were you, I'd come along on Christmas Eve to watch it. You might be surprised. These women aren't monsters, you know.'

'Maybe I will.'

Justin drifted away in search of a refill and Tony said, 'So how are you and Dani doing?'

'Not too bad, considering everything that's happened.'

Tony raised an eyebrow. 'Everything? You mean the burglary?'

'Yeah, well, that and . . .' He stopped. He'd had a few glasses of wine himself and it seemed Justin's wasn't the only tongue that had been loosened by alcohol.

'And?'

Noel was overcome by the urge to tell someone what was going on. 'We had some weird parcels, including a sexy Santa outfit. Dani had a creepy message too. Other stuff. The thing is . . . we think it was Alan.'

'Alan? Why?'

'Because the third parcel contained something that only Alan knew would freak us out.'

'What was it?'

'I can't say.' He didn't want Dani to kill him. 'But I'm keeping my eye on him.'

Tony ran a hand through his thick white hair. 'So that's what you wanted to talk to him about the other night? Wow. Well, I have to tell you, it doesn't sound like the kind of thing he'd do, although I guess everyone has their dark side. Their secret side. A friend of mine, another guy on the council, the most strait-laced guy you could ever meet, was caught dogging last year.' He sipped his wine. 'Alan, though. Want me to have a word with him?'

'No! I really don't want to accuse him if he's innocent.' Noel was flooded with regret. 'Oh God, I shouldn't have said anything.'

Tony patted his shoulder. 'Your secret's safe with me.'

Noel left the kitchen and went off in search of Alan. He was wasting his opportunity to spend time with him and assess his behaviour.

He found him in the garden, chatting with Zoe, who had a cornered look in her eye.

'It all sounds fascinating,' Alan was saying to Zoe, and Noel noticed that he was talking directly to her boobs. Was that because he was several inches shorter than her? Noel didn't think so. He seemed transfixed. He also, like half the people here, was clearly already drunk. His eyes were glassy and he seemed a little unsteady on his feet.

'Zoe was explaining TikTok to me,' Alan said. 'I did look at it once. It mainly seemed to be teenage girls doing stupid dances.'

There was something in the way he said 'teenage girls'. A hint of disgust. Was that what Noel and Dani were dealing with here? A misogynist who lusted after young women while also despising them? That, surely, was the kind of man who would get off on scaring Dani.

'I get so tired hearing people criticize social media,' Zoe said. 'There's so much creativity on there. Activism too.'

'You mean all that woke nonsense? I remember when—'

'Let's go and find Linda,' Noel said, escorting Alan away. Zoe mouthed 'Thank you' at Noel as he guided Alan towards the house.

'Linda. My lovely wife. Almost as lovely as yours.'

Noel stopped walking. 'What do you mean by that?'

How much had Alan had to drink? Noel guessed he must have started before he got here. His voice, when he replied, was slurred. 'You're so lucky.

146

Even if she won't wear a Santa outfit for you. Gotta say, she's looking good in that LBD tonight. Lucky man. Lucky, *lucky* man.' He belched. 'Hang on, I need to use your loo.'

He staggered away towards the downstairs toilet, leaving Noel feeling both dumbstruck and certain: Alan was the culprit. He wanted to call him out on it now, warn him that if he did anything else Noel would not be held responsible for his actions. But would it even sink in when the other man was so wasted?

He needed to talk to Dani. He found her in the dining room, chatting with a small group of neighbours, who Noel only vaguely recognized, about her job.

Noel took Dani's elbow and gently steered her over to the corner.

'I'm sure it's Alan,' he said, telling her about Alan's lascivious and icky behaviour. 'He had Zoe trapped in the garden. I thought I was going to have to surgically remove his eyes from her boobs.'

'Where is he now?'

'In the loo. We should wait till tomorrow, though, when he's sober. Go round there, tell him if he doesn't back off we're going to the police.'

'I don't know. If you're sure it's him, I think we should do it now.'

Noel didn't agree. 'I don't want to cause a massive scene in front of all our neighbours.'

They were all here. The whole of Nightingale Crescent and the adjoining streets, all named after great Brits. Noel didn't want to be forever remembered as the bloke who had called out his neighbour at a Christmas party. 'Let's do it tomorrow.'

Dani clenched her fists. 'I don't even like him being here, in our house. But you're right. If he's pissed, it's better to wait. But you have to promise me – you'll do it first thing tomorrow.'

'I promise.'

Noel was about to walk off when Dani said, 'While I've got you, you should say a few words. Thank everyone for chipping in to the collection.'

'Good idea. I'll go and start rounding people up.'

Noel went into the kitchen and garden and asked everyone to gather in the dining room, while Dani did the same in the living room. There was no sign of Alan; presumably he was still in the toilet. Zoe was in the kitchen talking to Justin, who seemed as transfixed by her as Alan had been. Zoe was smiling too. Were they flirting? Noel didn't think

Justin was Zoe's type – he seemed too introverted and nerdy for her – but people make unexpected choices at Christmas parties.

'Going to make a speech?' Tony asked, following Noel. Linda was there too, looking around like she was trying to locate her husband, and all their other neighbours. More and more people crowded into the room; so many he couldn't see all their faces.

He found a chair to stand on so everyone could see him and waited for everyone to quieten down. He looked over the sea of heads, searching for Dani, who waved at him.

'Hello, everyone,' he said. The assembled party goers, lubricated by alcohol, kept chatting. Noel tried again, with the same result.

'Hey!' Justin called out, his voice booming. Presumably this was his 'prison order' voice. 'Let the guy speak.'

'Thank you,' said Noel, once everyone had fallen silent. A crowd of faces, all looking at him. 'I promise I won't be long. I just want to—'

He heard the clunk first. Or maybe it was a popping sound.

And then all the lights went out.

17

Somebody gasped, and then someone else laughed, a high-pitched nervous sound ringing out in the darkness. Almost immediately, one of the younger people had the wherewithal to switch on the torch on their phone, and then everyone else followed suit, filling the room with spots of white light that joined together to create an unearthly glow.

Noel switched his own phone torch on and jumped down from the chair, pushing his way through the crowd towards the window. The exterior Christmas lights were off too, but the other houses on the street were still illuminated. So it was only their house that had the power cut.

A shiver went through him. After everything, he couldn't help but feel someone had done this deliberately. That it was sabotage.

Suddenly, there was someone in his personal space, breathing booze that almost knocked him backwards. It was Alan.

'It's your dodgy electrics again,' he said. 'Don't worry, I'll fix it.'

He vanished back into the crowd of bodies and Noel went to follow him, but suddenly Dani was there in front of him. She was breathing heavily, and in the strange, white light she looked awful, like a ghost condemned to haunt parties for eternity. There was a babble all around them, and the power cut added a frisson of excitement that would mean people would never forget this gathering.

'It's okay,' Noel said to Dani. 'Alan's gone to fix it. Although I need to go after him. He's so drunk I'm not sure he's capable.'

'It's not the power,' she said, grabbing his arm and stopping him from moving away. 'I got another message, just now. When I turned on the torch on my phone I saw that I had a message. WhatsApp this time.'

'What does it say?'

She handed him her phone so he could read it. If he already felt cold, this was like having ice injected straight into his veins.

It was a photo of the doll, followed by another message:

Why won't you play with me?

This was followed by a crying emoji. Then another message had arrived a couple of minutes later:

I left you a present in the basement. xx

There was a crying with laughter emoji, and then a Santa emoji and a skull. Strangely, there was a bird emoji too. A crow? No. It was black and white. A magpie.

Dani was squeezing his arm so hard it hurt. Later, he would find bruises where her fingertips had dug in.

'Did you just say Alan was going into the basement to fix the lights?'

'Oh God. Where's Linda? We have to deal with this now,' said Noel.

The house was still pitch black. If Alan was actually trying to resolve the problem, he wasn't having any success. Noel tried to reach the door of the dining room, to get to the hallway and the basement, but there were so many people blocking his path. He shouldered his way through a tightly packed group of his neighbours and found himself face to face with Tony and Justin, both of whom were holding their phones with their torches on, lighting up their faces and making them look like that skull emoji.

'Everything all right?' Tony asked.

'I need to get to the basement. Urgently.'

'No problem.' He raised his voice, turning towards the door. 'Move aside! We're coming through!'

It was like he was a celebrity being escorted through an airport by a pair of bodyguards. Noel reached the hallway, with Dani behind him. It was dark and empty – everyone who wasn't still in the dining room had gone into the lounge or the kitchen or the garden – and Noel went straight to the basement door, opening it and calling, 'Alan?'

There was no response.

'Hello? Alan?'

He went through the door and shone his phone torch down the stairs.

There was a dark shape on the basement floor below.

Noel hurried down, almost tripping as he went. Above him, he heard a woman's voice, Linda's, say, 'What's going on? Where's my husband?' and Dani, replying, 'He's down there.'

Noel could see what had happened before he reached the bottom of the steps. Could see it but couldn't quite believe it. Later, Dani would tell him she'd heard him make a horrible groaning noise, one he didn't remember making. Right now, all he was aware of was Linda coming down towards him, saying, 'Is he here? Alan?'

He was here. But he wasn't trying to fix the power cut. He wasn't doing anything but lying on the floor, completely still, his neck twisted at a horrible angle.

Beside him, ghastly in the light cast by Noel's torch, lay the doll.

Linda screamed.

18

There were still loads of people milling around in the house, although someone had found and lit some candles, as if they were at a vigil, the body still warm in the basement, or some sort of ghoulish Midnight Mass, the candle flames flickering in the draught from the front door.

Tony had taken Linda into the kitchen and given her a glass of brandy; she sat there staring into space, apparently in shock. Dani was outside, refusing to be in the house with the body or the doll. Zoe sat with her, draping a blanket over Dani's shoulders and trying to comfort her while Noel paced up and down the hallway, chewing his nails and wondering what had happened to his perfect Christmas. The presents, the messages, the burglary – and now, the blood-spattered icing on his Christmas cake, there was a dead man in his basement. On top of that, the doll was back. At least that proved, though he took no comfort from it, that he hadn't been paranoid in the woods.

Someone had been following him. That someone presumably being Alan.

What had been his plan? Noel assumed Alan had switched off the electricity, before sending the message to Dani and then volunteering to go into the basement, where he would 'fix' it and leave the doll. Unfortunately for Alan, this plan had gone wrong and he had slipped down the stairs while holding the doll.

But what had Alan been hoping to achieve? Was he trying to make himself look like a hero? Win their trust? Noel didn't get it. If Alan wanted to freak them out, all he had to do was switch off the electricity and leave the doll in the basement, then wait for Noel or Dani to find it when they went down to investigate.

The police arrived. It was the same pair who had come the other night, after the burglary: PCs Degville and Mayhew. They took one look at the body then called an ambulance and an emergency electrician.

'Tell us what happened,' Degville said, while Mayhew went into the kitchen to talk to Linda. Noel explained everything, including his theory that Alan had been the one to turn off the power. He spoke quietly, not wanting Linda to overhear.

'And he must have fished that doll out of the dumpster and—'

Degville stopped him. 'I think I'm going to need you to make a full statement about all of this. But you're basically saying you believe the deceased was harassing you.'

'Yes. He's the only person who knew about the doll.'

As he said this, Zoe came in to tell him that the electrician had arrived. Noel followed her outside then showed the electrician where the basement door was.

'Hang on,' he said. 'You want me to go down there, in the dark, with a dead body?'

Luckily, the ambulance pulled up at that exact moment and, as Alan's body was carried out, Linda emerged from the kitchen, weeping. Noel found himself staring at her, wondering if she would still weep when she found out what her husband had been up to.

The electrician, muttering something about how he was going to charge triple for this, went down into the basement.

Tony, who was looking after Linda, took her outside and led her towards her house, an arm around her shoulders. Noel watched them go, then became aware that someone was saying his name. It was Zoe.

'Noel, I think—'

At that moment the lights came on, and seconds later the electrician appeared, rubbing his hands together. PC Mayhew reappeared too.

'Someone removed the fuse from the fuse box,' the electrician said. 'Easy to fix.'

'But deliberate?' Degville asked.

'Oh yeah. I've never known a fuse to dematerialize on its own.' The electrician chortled to himself.

He went to walk away, but Noel said, 'Excuse me. Is it something anyone could do? Or would you need to be a trained electrician?'

'Well, it's not something we would ever recommend. But it would be pretty easy to learn to do. There are probably videos on YouTube. It's dangerous, though.' Sensing that he had an audience interested in his expertise, he launched into an explanation of how to remove a fuse, how to replace it, why you shouldn't do it, with numerous references to 'regs'. Noel thought it sounded like brain surgery, but he knew Alan was good at that sort of stuff.

Zoe was still trying to get his attention, but then

Dani called him from outside and he went out to her. By this point, the remaining party-goers were all on the lawn. Linda and Tony and Justin had all gone, and the ambulance had driven away.

Noel went over to Dani.

'Where's the doll?' she whispered.

'It must still be in the basement.'

'I need you to get it out and destroy it. I mean, completely destroy it. Not just throw it away. Burn it, crush it, smash it to pieces, whatever – then throw it away, somewhere a long way from here.'

Noel hesitated.

'But what if the police need to keep it as evidence?'

'Of what?'

'I don't know. Proof that Alan was harassing us. Did you take a screenshot of the message he sent you earlier?'

'No. But I don't see that it matters now. He's dead.' She got to her feet. 'I need to go and check on Mogwai. She's been up there on her own for hours. But please – get the doll out of the house first.'

Noel went inside, and straight down into the basement. He wasn't sure if he was imagining the cold, but he knew this part of the house would never seem the same. He would always see Alan's broken body right here on the hard floor.

He found a scarf in a box of old clothes that needed to be sent to the charity shop and wrapped the doll in it, not wanting to touch it. It stared up at him, eyes wide open. The way things were going, he'd soon have an aversion to dolls too. Pediophobia, it was called. The fear of inanimate objects that look like people. Why had he ever blabbed to Alan about Dani's phobia?

Back outside, he discovered that Zoe had gone, and the rest of the neighbours had dispersed. Only the police were still there, though they were about to leave.

'If you can come into the station tomorrow, we can take that statement.'

Noel nodded and watched them drive away.

He turned – and jumped. Dani was standing just inside the front door. She looked more stricken than she had when they'd found Alan's body.

'Look,' she said, holding out her phone.

There was a new message in her inbox.

Poor guy, such a shame. But you look so pretty when you're scared, Dani.

PS Tell Noel I've got a special present to give him on his birthday. It's going to be a Christmas he'll never forget.

Love Secret Santa aka The Christmas Magpie xx

'The Christmas Magpie? What the hell?'

'Noel, you're missing the most important part.'

Noel looked at the phone, then back at Dani, then at the phone again, not understanding what she meant. Until he saw the time stamp.

The message had been sent ten minutes ago. An hour after Alan's death.

19

Noel drove to the police station, going over everything in his head as he manoeuvred through the early-afternoon traffic. They had been wrong about Alan. He had been an innocent man. Someone else had sent the presents and messages. That person had probably also been responsible for the burglary, and for sabotaging the fuse box during the party. And a chilling, sickening question crept into his mind: had that person pushed Alan down the steps?

Were they, on top of everything else, a murderer?

Dani was back home, still in bed, having taken a sleeping pill at some point during the night, needing to knock herself out. Noel had left her there, looking peaceful, lost in what he hoped was a pleasant dream, with Mogwai curled up on the quilt, purring.

He pulled up in the police station's car park and got the doll, that evil boomerang of a doll, out of the boot. Dani had asked him to destroy it, but he had decided it would be wiser to take it to the police. It was evidence.

This was not, he thought as he entered the station, how he had intended to spend his birthday. And even if it hadn't been his birthday, it wasn't the best way to spend Christmas Eve. He should have been relaxing, wrapping some last-minute presents, making sure they had everything they needed for tomorrow's lunch. Instead, the house was still a mess after the party, Dani was traumatized and he had no idea what was going to happen next. In the most recent message, their tormentor had said he was going to give Noel a Christmas he would never forget. What did that mean? Was it a threat? Were they actually in danger? And what was all this weird Christmas Magpie stuff? If whoever was doing this had pushed Alan down the steps to his death, was he planning to do the same to Noel?

He quickened his pace. Hopefully the police would be able to sort things out. Or to reassure him, at least.

As he was about to enter the station, his phone buzzed. It was Zoe.

Are you free to talk?

He put the phone back into his pocket. He'd call her afterwards.

He asked to see if PC Degville was available, and the guy behind the desk went to find her while Noel waited. He was holding the doll, still wrapped in the scarf he'd found in the basement. He imagined himself saying, *Take her. Lock her up and throw away the key.* He rubbed at his face. He was feeling a little hysterical.

Degville arrived and asked him to follow her to a little room, where he placed the doll on the wooden desk between them.

'I don't know if you can test this for DNA or . . .'

He trailed off. Degville was staring at him.

'I mean, it keeps turning up. Whoever has done all of this has definitely touched it numerous times. The murderer, I mean.'

Degville looked taken aback. 'Murderer?'

'Yes. I think someone pushed Alan down the steps.'

Degville pushed her hair out of her eyes. 'The witnesses we spoke to last night, including Alan's wife, told us he was inebriated. "Pissed as a fart," according to one guy I spoke to.'

'Yes, that's true, but—'

'The steps down into the basement are steep, and it was dark. I think it would be easy to fall down them in those circumstances. Did you see anyone come out of the basement?'

'No, but I was trapped in the dining room.'

Degville sighed. 'Do you have the messages that were sent to Dani?'

Noel grimaced. 'No. Whoever sent them deleted them fifteen minutes after they were received. I thought Dani had taken screenshots last night, but she was in such a state that she forgot. The accounts used were clearly spam accounts. The profile pic was a Santa hat and the username was a string of numbers and letters.'

Degville wrote this down in her pad. 'Do you have any enemies?' she asked.

'No! Not that I know of, anyway. Dani's ex is a bit of a dickhead, but he lives in Ireland. I never fall out with anyone.'

'You haven't argued with any of your neighbours?'

'No. Everyone seems so nice. They had a whip-round after we were burgled, which was why we threw the party, to thank them.' He paused. Did he really want to say this? 'There's one guy who lives across the street who seems a bit creepy. Justin. He was there when Dani was talking about the Santa outfits and I thought he was watching us later that night, though he got very upset when I mentioned that.'

'Did he? You mean, angry?'

'Yeah, kind of.'

'Was he at the party?'

'Yes. He's actually a prison officer. Works at Franklin Grange.'

Degville bristled, as if he was accusing one of her colleagues of something. But she wrote his name down then got to her feet. 'Thank you for coming in.'

'Is that it?'

A raised eyebrow.

'Do you think we're in danger? The message from last night – they said they were going to give me a Christmas I'd never forget.'

Degville looked sad, as if Noel wasn't understanding something simple. 'I'm afraid there isn't very much we can do at the moment, although I can assure you we will look into everything you've told me. And regarding Alan's death, we might have to wait for the coroner's report.'

'How long will that be?'

She didn't answer directly. 'For now, the best thing to do is keep a log of everything that happens, and if either of you receive any more messages, let us know, especially if they are threatening in any way.'

'But . . .'

'It's Christmas Eve. Go home, try to relax. We'll be in touch.'

He left the station almost bursting with frustration. They were useless. How was he supposed to relax? At least they had the doll now, although Dani wouldn't be happy he hadn't destroyed it.

Getting back into the car, Noel remembered the text from Zoe. He called her and she picked up straight away.

'How's Dani today?' she asked.

'She was still asleep when I left. I've just been to make a statement to the police. Not that they're going to do anything this side of Christmas.' He put her on speakerphone and left the car park, heading back towards Nightingale Crescent. It was mid-afternoon now and the roads were busy, as all the people who'd had to go into offices today knocked off early and headed home. Noel had a churning sensation in his belly, the message Dani had received playing on repeat in his head: *Tell Noel I've got a special present to give him on his birthday.*

'Noel, are you still there?'

'Oh God. Sorry. I was miles away. What was it you wanted to talk to me about?'

Zoe said, 'I kept trying to tell you last night, but there were constant interruptions. You said that Alan was the only person who could have known about Dani's fear of dolls, but that isn't true.'

'What do you mean?'

'I only remembered last night, during the party, but a couple of years ago, when Dani started at the agency, Phil used to make us appear in loads of videos, trying to create clips that would go viral on TikTok and Insta.'

He knew this already. This was when they were trying to build a reputation for being creative, before they used influencers and stopped getting their own staff to film themselves.

'There was a video we all made where we had to talk about our biggest fears. I think we were trying to promote a horror movie. It was definitely something Halloween-related, anyway. And you probably know what I'm going to say.'

The churning in his stomach had been replaced by a blast of ice. 'Dani talked about her fear of dolls.'

'Yes. Specifically, porcelain dolls. Everyone else said things like spiders and wasps and balloons . . .

but Dani was really funny in it, talking about how if she was Prime Minister dolls would be banned. She's obviously completely forgotten that she did it because we made hundreds of videos around that time. Sometimes dozens a day. She might not even know that it was posted, but it was. And if you scroll all the way back, it's still there, available for anyone to watch.'

Noel was silent, and Zoe filled it by saying, 'I thought you should know. The person who sent the doll – it could literally be anyone. As long as they know where Dani works.'

He groaned, then said, 'Do you want to come round? Have a drink with us?'

'I can't. I'm on my way to Franklin Grange.'

'For their Christmas performance?'

'Yes. Exciting, eh? You know I was talking to Justin at your party? He told me they were inviting people from local government and businesses and so on. Gave me an email address. I think one of your other neighbours is going. Tony, is it?'

'You want to spend Christmas Eve in a prison? Wait. Is something going on with you and Justin? Is this his warped idea of a date?'

Zoe laughed. 'He did mention something about going for a drink afterwards.'

'Oh my God, Zoe. He's weird. In fact—'

'What?'

'How do we know it wasn't him who pushed Alan down the stairs?'

Zoe responded immediately. 'He was standing right next to me. He didn't leave my sight.'

This was new information. Noel should relay it to the police. It took him a second to realize Zoe was still talking.

'. . . don't need to worry about me. To be honest, the main reason I'm going is I want to see the famous Lucy Newton.'

'Well, stay safe. Don't get too close to her.'

Zoe laughed again. 'I won't. And please, look after Dani. Tell her I'll be in touch later.'

She hung up. Suddenly feeling sick and dizzy, and unsafe to drive, he pulled over in a lay-by and picked up his phone, opening Instagram and navigating to Dani's agency's account. He scrolled back. It took ages, but eventually he got back to Halloween 2022, and there it was: the clip of Dani and a few of her colleagues talking about what scared them. Dani was even tagged in the post.

Anyone could have searched for her and discovered her greatest fear.

Anyone.

20

Noel needed to think, so drove around for a little while. Passing a pub on a country lane a few miles from home, he saw a group of revellers emerge, all wearing Santa hats, weaving around as they walked off towards the nearby village. How he wished he was one of them. Carefree. Merry. Instead, he was going crazy, convinced he had a massive target on his back, with no idea why.

He hadn't been lying when he told PC Degville he never fell out with anyone. He didn't have enemies. He never argued with people on Facebook. He didn't have a nemesis, as far as he was aware. Dani, although less of a people-pleaser than him, was the same. They led quiet lives, getting on with building their nest, wrapped up in each other. They didn't blast loud music through open windows, or steal their neighbours' parking spots, or get into road rage incidents. They didn't have a noisy dog. They didn't even let their cat out to crap in other people's gardens.

They were, even though Noel didn't like to admit it, completely ordinary.

How could they be the subjects of a campaign like this one? Something that wasn't blatant or big enough to make the police spring into rapid action, but that undermined their happiness, put them on edge, played on their fears and their insecurities. How could they ever be happy again in their brand-new home? The violation of the burglary had been bad enough, but now a man had died there – and perhaps, in fact Noel was increasingly convinced, it had been murder. But by the time the police figured that out, if they ever did, the aggressor might be long gone.

Again, he thought about the message Dani had received. The promise of a 'special present'.

What if Noel's special present was Secret Santa doing something awful to Dani?

This thought sent a new wave of sickness through him.

He needed to get home. Now.

He ran through the front door, fear coursing through him, skin prickling with dread.

'Dani?' He called her name but got no response.

Convinced he was going to find Dani's corpse

176

in their bedroom, he ran up the stairs, shouting her name and finding Mogwai on the landing, standing outside the closed bedroom door. Noel stood there for a second, swaying, too afraid to open the door because he was terrified that when he did, this would be the moment his life would change. From the moment he went into the bedroom his life would divide into two: the Before and the After.

A noise came from the other side of the door. A groan.

He burst through, almost blind with panic, and found Dani half dressed, her hair wet where she had obviously just got out of the shower. She was groaning because the cord of her hair dryer was tangled with the one from her hair straighteners.

'Oh, thank God!' He grabbed her and pulled her into a tight hug, her hair cold against his cheek. 'Why was the door shut, with Mogwai outside?'

She broke free of his embrace. She was still holding the hair dryer. 'You know she tries to get into the shower and then goes mental when I dry my hair. I always shut her out.'

'Of course. Yes.'

'What is it, Noel? Has something else happened? Oh please, I can't take anything else.'

'It's okay. Calm down.'

'Don't tell me to calm down! Especially when you're about as a calm as a tornado!'

'I'm sorry.' He took a deep breath, in, then out. 'Please sit.'

She sat on the bed and he joined her there, taking a few more breaths before updating her on everything. The visit to the police and their reaction to what he'd told them, and the conversation with Zoe.

As he told her what Zoe had said, the colour drained from Dani's face. She found her phone, which was plugged in beside the bed, and scrolled through her account, watching the same video Noel had watched a little while ago. As she watched it, he noticed that dusk was creeping across the estate. The whole day, his birthday, had vanished. But maybe it could still be rescued. Maybe they could find out who was behind all of this and put a stop to it. Now that would be the perfect present.

'I forgot all about this,' Dani said. 'We were making so many clips back then, and you and I had just got engaged, and my nan was in hospital after her stroke, do you remember? There was so much going on.'

'It's okay. I can hardly remember what I did

last week.' Apart from get burgled, dump a doll in the woods while being followed, almost start a fist fight with an innocent neighbour who had ended up dying in their basement. 'But I wanted to ask you something. I went through and couldn't see anything, but have you posted anything about your hatred of sexy Santa outfits?'

'No.'

'Are you a hundred per cent sure?'

She thought about it. 'Yes. It's not even a deep-seated thing that I've always carried round with me. I'm not sure I'd even thought about it until that day.'

'Okay. So that means it has to be someone who was there that evening. We assumed it was Alan listening in, and I suspected Justin, but Zoe just told me he was standing next to her when Alan was pushed down the stairs. Who else was at the switch-on?'

'Linda, remember? She said she felt sorry for you.' She sucked in air. 'I thought she must have gone home and told Alan about it later, but oh God, Noel, what if it was *all* Linda? The pies. The dress. The doll. Everything else.'

They both stared at each other. Linda? Had they suspected the wrong half of that married couple?

'It can't be her,' Noel said. 'She's the principal

of a posh girls' school. The head of the residents' association.'

'I'd say that makes her more likely to be guilty. Everyone knows psychopaths and narcissists gravitate towards positions of power.'

'But . . . she's a woman.'

Dani shook her head. 'Noel, we live a few miles from a women's prison. A prison that houses Lucy Newton. You know the things she did to her neighbours. I read the news reports about her, and they all talked about how she and her husband hid in plain sight, pretending to be upstanding members of the community. She murdered eighteen people in that care home where she worked.'

'Linda.' Noel shivered. 'You think . . . she might have pushed her own husband to his death?'

'She would have known he'd volunteer to go down and deal with the power outage. Maybe she'd been looking for a way to get rid of him for ages. If she is a psycho like Lucy.'

'I've just thought of something else,' Noel said.

Dani made a pained noise.

'Do you remember, Linda told us that Alan said Justin hadn't captured anything on his security cameras. What if she was just saying that so we wouldn't ask him to check?'

'Oh my God.'

'He might have footage of her leaving the parcels on our doorstep.'

Dani stood up. 'We need to go over and ask him to look.'

Mogwai, who was sitting on the carpet licking his paws, watched them as they talked. Her tail was thick and she seemed uneasy, just as she had when the packages had been delivered.

'We can't now,' Noel said. 'He's at work, remember?'

'In that case, let's go and talk to Linda.'

'And accuse her? I don't think that's wise. If she really is guilty, that means she's dangerous.'

'I don't care.' Dani was pulling the rest of her clothes on, putting a woolly hat on over her wet hair. 'She's not going to do anything to us in the middle of the street, is she?'

She marched past him and Noel followed her down the stairs. She slipped her trainers on and Noel hurried to do the same. Then he was chasing her up the street and standing behind her as she hammered on Linda's door, just as he had done when he had thought Alan had sent the doll.

A grey-haired woman came out of the house to the left. She had been at the lights switch-on and their party. She was in her sixties, he guessed. What was her name? Val, that was it.

'She's not in.' Noel felt the uncanny touch of déjà vu. 'She's at the prison.'

'Her as well?' Dani said.

Val rolled her eyes. 'Some big show they're putting on at the taxpayers' expense. To be honest, I was shocked when I saw Linda come out earlier. Not exactly playing the grieving widow. Poor Alan.'

Noel thanked her for her help and was about to walk away when he noticed that she had a security camera above her front door.

'Does that thing actually work?' he asked.

'Of course.'

He followed the direction of the camera. It pointed down the road, straight towards Noel and Dani's house.

'Is it on all the time? Or just motion-triggered?'

Val narrowed her eyes, like she was wondering why he was asking all these questions. But she seemed a little lonely, like she didn't get to chat to many people.

'It's on all the time. It tapes over itself – is that the right phrase? – every fourteen days.'

'And you can see our front door on the footage?'

'I'm not spying on you.'

Noel smiled. 'I didn't think you would be. But I'm sure you heard about our burglary?'

'I chipped in to the collection.'

'Of course. Thank you. I was wondering if your camera captured anything.'

Val shook her head. 'I already checked.'

'That's great. But would you mind if we took a look? We've had a few odd things happen recently, and it would be really helpful.'

Val didn't even need to think about it. It was Christmas Eve, she was on her own, and here was an opportunity to talk about her favourite topic: nefarious goings-on in the neighbourhood. 'Of course. Come in.'

21

The big day was here. Finally. The plot Lucy had concocted with Hell's Belle would be, literally, acted out. Mayhem would break out in the prison. Patricia would be appalled, the other women would no doubt find the whole thing hilarious – far more entertaining than the morality play they were supposed to be consuming – and Lucy would have plausible deniability because Helen had agreed to take all the blame/credit.

She thought back to her initial conversation with Helen, when Lucy had still been working on her adaptation.

'You want to get out of here, don't you?' Lucy had said. 'Get yourself transferred somewhere . . . less soft.'

'Too right. I'm sick of this place. It's full of cry babies. Present company excepted.'

Lucy had approximated a smile. 'How would you feel about causing some chaos on stage?'

Lucy had laid out the plan as quickly as she

could, knowing how rapidly Helen got bored. Lucy would write two versions of her script: the official one, in which Emma Liza Scrooge learned the error of her ways, yawn yawn; and a secret version, where Scrooge told the Ghost of Christmas Yet To Come where to go before flinging Bobbi, played by Andrea, off the stage into Patricia's lap. That would be the cue for Helen's lackeys, all of whom were in the audience, primed, to kick off. Storm the stage, smash up the props, pull down the curtains, grab all the mince pies and drink that had been laid out and start a massive food fight. In the midst of the chaos, Helen and her biggest sidekicks were going to grab one of the male officers – Justin Graves would be perfect – drag him on stage and make him dance like the stripper they had asked for.

If that didn't get Helen transferred, nothing would.

So why, now, did Lucy feel so low?

It was because the project she had been working on through December was almost over, and, beyond that, the great tedious greyness of prison life stretched ahead of her. A new year would arrive, and it would be exactly the same as this one. No light at the end of her tunnel.

Even her Secret Santa had turned out to be a disappointment. She had grabbed Andrea this morning, hoping there might be a final card before Christmas, but Andrea had shrugged and said, 'Sorry, nothing.'

What if she never heard from this person again? Never found out what they had done, or what they had planned? Surely she wouldn't hear from them once Christmas had passed?

All of this had put her in an extremely bad mood.

Not helped by Camilla asking her to help set everything up. Surely the writer shouldn't have to get her hands dirty? She couldn't say no, though, so around lunchtime, she wandered down to the hall. As she approached, she could hear a hubbub of voices and, entering, she saw Patricia with a large group. These, Lucy assumed, were the visiting VIPs. People from the local community, nearby businesses, the council, and so on. Patricia wanted them to see the great work she was doing here; that this wasn't just a holiday camp for bad girls. Losers, Lucy thought. Imagine wanting to spend the day before Christmas in a place like this.

There were around two dozen of them, a mix of ages and genders. Most of them were smartly dressed, in suits, with a couple wearing stupid jumpers with snowmen or reindeer on. A hideous trend, in Lucy's opinion. As she walked over to talk to Camilla, who was on the stage, she felt all their necks swivel. There was an attractive young woman with light red hair. A middle-aged woman and a man with a snowy thatch, both goggling at her.

She could almost read their thoughts. *It's her. The infamous Dark Angel.*

She didn't acknowledge their existence, just concentrated on what Camilla was saying.

'Are you excited?' Camilla asked.

'Hmm.'

The teacher frowned. 'What's the matter?'

Lucy gritted her teeth. 'I suppose I'm sad that it's almost over.'

'I am a little, too. But I've got a nice surprise for you. Patricia said that as we work so well together, and because I believe you have so much talent, she wants me to come back in the new year. She wants you to help me run creative writing classes for the other women. Won't that be fun!'

It took all of Lucy's willpower to stop herself from saying, 'I'd rather stab myself in the eye with a broken bauble.' Instead, she said, 'So much fun.'

Camilla beamed. 'We're going to have a blast, Lucy. Maybe we can adapt another Dickens next.

Oliver Twist, perhaps? Or we could do something more challenging. A modern Shakespeare retelling, perhaps. Or maybe even write something completely original. What do you think?'

'Maybe a murder mystery.'

'Perhaps not that.'

Camilla clapped Lucy on the shoulder, and again Lucy had to engage maximum willpower to stop herself from grabbing Camilla's hand and snapping all her fingers.

They got on with setting up the stage, working in what Camilla no doubt thought was companionable silence, while Lucy continued to think about her Secret Santa, imagining the things they might be doing out there to wreck someone's holidays. As she daydreamed, she noticed that one of the visitors kept looking over at her. She was the middle-aged woman she had spotted earlier, wearing a blue suit. She overheard Patricia tell someone else that the woman was the headmistress of a local girls' school. She looked very cosy with the white-haired guy.

Justin was there too, and he also kept glancing over at Lucy. He was really starting to give her the ick, like a puppy that wanted too much attention. Perhaps she should tell Patricia that he had propositioned her, tried to follow her into the showers, something like that. Get him fired. That would be fun.

After a while, the group left for a tour of the prison. Lucy got on with preparing for the play, ensuring the props were in place and the lights were working, and then helping to lay out the food and drink.

'All done,' she said at last.

Camilla, who had also been putting mince pies on plates and filling plastic jugs with squash, gave her a thumbs-up. 'See you at four.'

Lucy headed back. There was a buzz in the halls. The women were excited, both the 'actors' who were taking part and those who were merely going to watch. Helen had hinted there was going to be a big surprise, something they would want to stay tuned for. Or perhaps they were simply looking forward to getting their teeth into a mince pie. Whatever, it was something different. Something to break the monotony. Lucy wasn't the only one who felt it – although, obviously, she experienced it more keenly, being more intelligent and in need of stimulation than anyone else here. *Different, special, better*, as someone Lucy used to know had said.

She reached her room – and froze in the doorway. There was something on the bed.

Another card.

She checked the hallway, then closed her door. This time the card was sealed and the envelope bore no stamp, just her name in block capitals. That was exciting: it had obviously been hand-delivered.

Did that mean whoever had been sending her these cards was here, in the prison?

Lucy tore it open. Again, it was a shop-bought card, and again it showed a pretty house, this time on a snowy street. But someone had drawn a magpie sitting on the house's roof, peering down the chimney with a glint of mischief in its eye.

Lucy opened the card and read the message:

My work is almost done – and I can't wait to show you everything.
Stay in your cell during the play and I will come and find you.
Secret Santa
aka The Christmas Magpie xx

Lucy's pulse rarely accelerated, so it took her a moment to recognize that sensation in her chest. The feeling of her heart beating hard. *The Christmas Magpie.* This was exciting. But how was she supposed to stay in her room? They would miss her in the hall if she didn't show up.

There was still an hour to go till the play was due to start, and Lucy paced back and forth. She had slipped the card beneath her pillow, but she kept taking it out and reading it.

She made a decision.

Four o'clock came and she headed back to the hall. All around her, women came out of their rooms and headed in the same direction. She saw Helen, who caught her eye and winked. Andrea, unaware of the fate that awaited her – being shoved off the stage – was smiley and chatty. They all filed into the hall and the actors headed to the backstage area while the other women filled the rows of seats, chattering and eyeing the food that was laid out at the edge of the room, which they weren't allowed to touch till after the performance. The VIPs were in their seats near the front.

Could it be one of them who had left the card? Were they her Santa, her magpie? She tingled with anticipation as she took a seat in the back row, right in the corner. If Camilla or Patricia tried to usher her forward she would tell them she preferred to watch from back here because she didn't want to distract anyone or take the spotlight away from the performers.

The moment arrived. Helen took the stage as

Scrooge, drawing a huge cheer from the assembled prisoners. She strutted around, acting out all the lines Lucy had written about how much she hated this season and setting up the story about her being a hardened criminal who was motivated by greed. Dickens, Lucy thought, would be spinning in his grave. *I truly am talented*, she thought. *Probably better than old Dickens himself.*

She waited until Marley's ghost appeared, dragging paper chains behind her, much to the mirth of the audience, and got up from her seat, slipping away and out of the hall. Everyone was so entranced by the play that they didn't even notice her go, though she assumed her Secret Santa would have been watching.

She hurried back to her room and waited.

Two minutes later, she heard footsteps coming along the corridor.

And then a hushed voice outside her room.

'Lucy? Are you there?'

'I'm here.'

An exhalation of excitement.

'Come on,' the voice said. 'Lucy – we're going to get you out of here.'

22

The security system was controlled via Val's computer, which was on a desk in her dining room. Noel saw that Val had been correct. The cameras transmitted footage to an app on her PC twenty-four hours a day, then looped and recorded over itself every two weeks.

Thankfully, the footage was captured in separate daily files, so he didn't need to search through one enormous video. Sitting at Val's desk, he went straight to the day of the burglary. That had been the sixteenth, a mere eight days ago, though it seemed much longer. They had gone to the cinema that evening and got home around ten thirty. They weren't sure exactly what time the burglary had taken place, but it must have been after dark, so Noel forwarded through until around four thirty, when they had both still been at work, and then scrubbed through more slowly, zooming in as close as he could on their front door. From this distance, the picture wasn't very clear, but he thought if someone looked right at the camera, and it was someone he knew, he might recognize them. At the very least, if he found that they had captured the burglar, he would be able to take this to the police. Surely they would have the technology to enhance the picture.

The person came into view at 20.35, appearing through the side gate. Behind Noel, Dani gasped, and Val exclaimed, 'Who's that?'

The person was dressed all in black and wearing a beanie hat. They had their head down so their face wasn't visible, and they stayed close to the wall.

Noel freeze-framed the image and zoomed in closer, though the picture became so blurry and pixellated that it was impossible to see who it was. Except . . .

'It's a woman,' he said.

'How can you tell that?' Val asked.

'Isn't it obvious? The body shape.' Linda, he thought. They were right about it being her.

Dani leaned in closer. 'I don't know. It could be a guy.'

They watched the person pick up the box from the doorstep, bending at the knee and then quickly retreating back through the side gate.

'What day was the doll left on our doorstep?' Noel asked Dani.

'I can't remember. No, wait. It was the day before that. The fifteenth. You put it in the bin that night and the bin men came the next morning.'

That was right. That morning, he had given Justin a lift to work.

'Okay, let's look at the fifteenth.'

'This is exciting, isn't it?' Val said. 'Do you know what? I could murder a sherry. Do you want one?'

'No, thank you,' Noel said, concentrating on forwarding slowly through the video file, watching the bin van roll down the road and stop outside their house.

Val returned from the kitchen. 'That's annoying. I don't have any. I think I brought my only bottle to your party.'

She shot Dani an accusatory look, as if she'd stolen Val's precious booze, and Dani said, 'It's still in our kitchen. I don't think anyone touched it.' She paused because Val was still staring at her. 'How long do you think this will take, Noel? I could always pop back and fetch it.'

'That would be lovely,' said Val.

Noel laughed, despite the tension that clawed at his insides. 'Go ahead. This could take a while because we don't know what time the parcel was left.'

'Okay. Can you give me your keys?'

Dani left and he heard the front door shut, leaving him with Val.

'Such a nice young woman,' she said. 'Unlike a lot of your generation, no offence. Always on their phones, staring at that TishTosh or whatever it's called.'

Noel tuned her out. He was too busy staring at the screen.

He'd been watching for someone to walk towards the house, either Linda going down the street from close to where the camera was situated, or Justin coming from across the street. So he didn't take much notice of the car pulling up outside their house at first. A little white car. It was only when someone walked up their driveway holding a parcel in front of them that he realized 'Secret Santa' had arrived in the vehicle.

Val saw it too and fell silent as Noel watched the person put the package on the doorstep, then turn and head back to their car. They were wearing the beanie again, but – to his great delight – they paused for a second and looked up the street, straight towards the camera.

He paused the footage and zoomed in, unable to believe what he was seeing. He knew that car.

'Well I never. You were right,' Val said. 'It *is* a woman. Definitely. Do you know her?'

Noel couldn't speak. Again, zooming in had pixellated the image, but the woman who had left them the doll, and presumably done everything else, was gazing straight into the camera, so it was easy to see who she was. It was a face he had seen many times before.

'Yeah,' he said. 'I do know her.'

23

'Come with me,' the woman said, appearing in the doorway. She was young, around thirty. The pretty redhead that Lucy had spotted earlier. She seemed calm, and Lucy immediately thought: *She's like me. She's one of us.* One of the people that society labels as psychopathic, like Lucy and Chris. A former room-mate of Lucy's, a woman called Fiona, had always said they were different, special, better.

Lucy caught her breath.

'Who are you?' she asked, not moving.

'You don't need to know that right now. I'll tell you when we're out. We need to hurry, while everyone is distracted and watching the play.'

'I'm not going anywhere until you at least tell me your name.'

The woman looked over her shoulder. 'Okay. It's Zoe.'

'Zoe.'

'Are you going to come with me?'

'You're Secret Santa? The Christmas Magpie?'

Zoe smiled. 'I thought you'd like that. Magpie. It's what they called you at your first trial. A magpie stealing happiness from others. Wrecking their nests.'

'And that's what you've been doing?'

'Yes. Stealing Christmas from this couple who you would absolutely hate.' Her eyes flashed. 'You're my heroine, Lucy. But please, we need to go before anyone notices you're not in the hall.'

She walked down the hall, faster than anyone ever walked at Franklin Grange, but Lucy was able to keep up easily.

'You're one of the VIPs?' she asked in a quiet voice.

'Yes. I'm here representing the company I work for. A social media agency.'

'And how exactly are we going to get out? Have you stolen a bunch of keys or something?'

Zoe smiled, though she didn't slow down. 'Not quite. We have help from someone who works here. A guard. His name's—'

'Justin.'

Zoe turned her head sharply towards her, surprised. 'Yes. How did you know that?'

'I've seen him looking at me.'

Zoe exhaled through her nose. 'He should have

202

been more careful. Someone might have noticed.'

Lucy thought about what Andrea had said and was tempted to tell this woman that other inmates *had* noticed. Instead, she said, 'I'm unusually observant.'

'Of course. You're an extraordinary person, Lucy. And you have a lot of friends on the outside. Fans, I guess you could call them. People who know how special you are, who don't care about what you did. It's your nature, isn't it? You can't help being how you are, and society needs to learn to respect that.'

'And Justin thinks that too?'

'Yes. He told me that after he started working here and met you, he began to dig more deeply into your background. He read the original version of your book and—'

'How? It was never published.'

'It leaked online. Apparently it was someone who worked for the literary agency that used to represent you. They uploaded it on to some pirate site. Anyway, Justin read it and then discovered our group. There aren't many of us.'

'Oh.'

'But we are small and passionate, and we believe you should be free, Lucy.' She smiled. 'Justin and

I have been chatting for months, planning this. And then . . . I don't know if you believe in seren- dipity, but I'd been looking for a target, someone to have some fun with. Then this woman I work with, who I pretend to be friends with, moved in opposite Justin with her new husband, and it struck me – they would be perfect. They're just like one of the couples you used to have fun tormenting.'

'And Justin knows what you've been up to?'

'Oh no. He doesn't have a clue about that part. No one does, except you. He's just agreed to help me get you out.'

They were almost at the end of the corridor now, where it divided in two. One corridor led to the hall and the other led towards the administra- tive block, beyond which lay the exit.

'This way,' Zoe said, heading right, towards the admin block, and they were about to vanish into that corridor when Lucy heard a voice.

'Lucy?'

It was Camilla, hurrying towards them from the direction of the hall. In the distance, Lucy heard the rumble of laughter. The play would be reach- ing its climax very soon, with Helen's surprise ending. It was as if Lucy had been in on Zoe's plan to break her out. When Hell's Belle got going, it would capture every eye and ear, making it even easier for Lucy to slip out.

Except Camilla was here to ruin everything.

'What are you doing?' she asked. 'You're missing the play. Who's this? What are you doing?'

'So many questions.'

Lucy glanced at Zoe, who had stopped walking, then took a step towards Camilla. They were very close to the entrance to the toilets, which made Lucy realize what she needed to do. 'Give me one minute,' she said to Zoe. 'I'll deal with her.'

'What are you doing?' Camilla asked, her voice catching with fear as Lucy grabbed her arm. 'Lucy, get off me.'

'Shut up.'

She pushed Camilla through the door into the toilets, then shoved her up against the tiled wall. She thought about how Camilla had patronized her, looked down on her and treated her like a child. She remembered Camilla's smile earlier when she'd told Lucy they would be continuing to work together. All those hours stretching ahead, in this awful woman's company. And it wasn't just contempt that drove Lucy now. It was Camilla's fear, coming off her in such strong waves Lucy could feel them. It energized her. Made her feel alive.

She pushed Camilla into one of the stalls and stepped inside. Camilla was so much weaker than Lucy. She cowered, trying to squirm away as Lucy put her hands around her skinny throat.

'Please, Lucy,' Camilla said, her voice raspy and pathetic. 'Please. It's Christmas.'

Lucy treated that plea with the contempt it deserved. She squeezed harder, and put her face close to Camilla's, staring into her bulging, terrified eyes.

'Bah humbug. Bitch.'

She emerged from the toilets a minute later, feeling better than she had in years, to find Zoe in an agitated state.

'We have to go,' Zoe said. 'Right this second.'

'Come on then. Lead the way.'

They hurried down the corridor that led to the admin block, and there at the end of the corridor was Justin, shifting from foot to foot, sweat gleaming on his brow, too shy and awkward to look at Lucy properly. He let them through one set of doors then led them quickly to another, unlocking it with a set of keys, and then they were walking across a yard past another building, Justin telling them to be silent, and there it was. The gate to the outside. He glanced around, and Lucy saw how much he was trembling. This fool. This mug. Didn't he know she would never return his admiration or adoration? If he got in her way, she would kill him without hesitation.

He unlocked the gate and said, 'I need to get back.'

'Thank you,' Zoe said. 'I owe you one.'

Justin looked at Lucy and said, 'Run free,' like she was a laboratory animal he was liberating. Then he turned and jogged back through the yard.

Lucy followed Zoe through the gate. Oh, how much sweeter the air tasted on this side. Somewhere in the distance, from inside the prison, Lucy heard a roar. Helen must have just switched into the alternative version of the play. Shoving Andrea off stage, trashing the set and grabbing a male guard – not Justin, because he was here, but one of the others. But there was no time to enjoy any of it. Zoe hurried her across the street where her car was parked, a little white Honda. They got in.

'Where are we going?' Lucy asked. 'Do you have a safe house? Somewhere for me to hide? Are you going to get me out of the country? What's the plan?'

'Yes, all of that. But first, I have to show you what I've been doing. It's time to finish it.' She grinned and started the engine. 'You're going to love it, Lucy. It's my tribute to you. My present.'

They had driven through the early-evening darkness for about five miles until they reached a new housing development. A quiet street with new-build houses, all with Christmas decorations lit up outside.

Zoe pulled up outside a house halfway down the street and motioned for Lucy to accompany her. She walked up to the front door and rang the bell.

Lucy didn't like this. She wanted to be somewhere safe, hidden. Maybe she should kill Zoe and take her car – but she didn't know where she would go. She hadn't had time to figure it out. So, for now, she was reliant on this woman she didn't know. This fellow psychopath.

And she had to admit, she was enjoying this. Like a cat that had been caged and denied access to mice for a long time, she was itching for the chance to use her claws.

The door opened and Lucy found herself look-ing at another attractive young woman who smiled at Zoe and then looked at Lucy with confusion.

'Hey, Dani,' Zoe said. 'I've got someone I'd like you to meet.'

Lucy saw it on Dani's face: her attempts to place Lucy, to figure out where she knew her from.

By the time she realized, it was too late.

24

'It's Zoe,' Noel said, standing up and moving away from Val's computer. He couldn't believe it. *Zoe?* Why would she have done all this? None of it made sense.

But of course, Zoe had known about Dani's fear of dolls, and Dani had no doubt told Zoe how much she disliked those Santa outfits. She would know when the house was empty, and she had been there at the party. Where had she been when the lights went out? He'd seen her in the kitchen with Justin, just before, but he hadn't seen her come into the dining room.

He had read all about this when he'd looked up Lucy Newton. Psychopaths hiding in plain sight, pretending to be normal, mimicking regular people with regular emotions. Lucy had got her kicks from targeting her neighbours and making their lives a misery. Was Zoe like that? Was that why she had told Noel about Dani's old social media clip? Because she wanted Dani to be scared of everyone?

What else had she planned?

Whatever it was, he had caught her. He had video evidence. But he knew Dani was going to be destroyed when he showed her. Speaking of which – where was she?

He left Val's dining room and went to the front door, opening it and looking down the street.

Zoe's car was parked outside his house.

'Call the police,' he shouted at Val as he flew through the door. 'Ask for PC Degville.'

The car was empty and the front door was shut. He felt his pockets for his keys then remembered he'd given them to Dani to let herself in to get the sherry. He rang the bell then hammered on the door with his fists.

'Dani!'

There was no response.

He found his phone and tried to call her, but it went straight to voicemail. What was going on in there? Was Zoe hurting his wife? And how long would it take the police to arrive?

He went through the side gate into the garden, peering through the French doors into the living room, which was empty, the lights off. 'Dani!' he shouted again. Then, 'Zoe. I know what you've been doing. Let's talk about it.'

He waited. Nothing.

Screw this.

There were some red bricks in the shed which had been left behind by the builders. He was going to do what the burglar – again, presumably Zoe – had done: smash the panel in the back door and let himself into the kitchen.

He crossed the lawn to the shed, found a brick and headed back to the house. There was one light on upstairs, the spare bedroom, though he couldn't see any sign of movement. His insides roiled with dread, his heartbeat pounding in his ears. What if Dani was already dead? Was Zoe waiting, crouched in the dark, for him to get home so she could murder him too?

He smashed the back door panel, reaching through to unlock the door and let himself in. He grabbed a knife from the kitchen block and headed into the hallway. He opened the basement door and peered down the steps. The light was on down there.

'Dani?' he called.

She responded. Oh, thank God. She was alive. 'Be careful. She's—'

There was a noise behind him. He tried to turn but didn't have time. He felt a pair of hands on his back, and then he was falling.

25

When he came to, he was lying on the floor of his basement. He couldn't move his hands, which were behind his back. They were, he realized, tied together with what felt like rope, rough against his wrists. His ankles were tied with rope too.

Zoe was standing over him. She was holding a small gun, which she pointed directly at Noel's chest.

'I'm so glad you came home,' she said. 'I thought I was going to have to do this without you.'

He turned his head. Dani was beside him, lying on her side with her own wrists secured behind her. And he could sense someone else in the room. He managed to shift his body weight so he could look behind him. There was a tall blonde woman.

She was also lying on her back with her wrists and ankles bound.

'Let me introduce you to Lucy Newton,' Zoe said.

'I'm going to kill you,' Lucy said to her, sounding unnaturally calm.

'Um, I don't think it's going to be that way round.'

'I've called the police,' Noel said.

'It's Christmas Eve,' Zoe said. 'The police who haven't already gone home to their families are going to be at Franklin Grange, trying to figure out where the hell Lucy has gone. They'll never think to look here. Not before I'm miles away anyway, and you're all dead.'

'You're on camera,' Noel said. 'The woman up the road, she has everything recorded.'

'I don't care, Noel. They're going to know it was me who helped Lucy get out of prison, but it's fine. I have a safe house.' She smiled at Lucy. 'Not for you, I'm afraid. For myself. I have friends who are going to help me get out of the country. It's all been planned. Christmas Day is the perfect day to escape, you know. Skeleton staff everywhere. Nobody paying much attention.'

'It's not as easy as you think,' Lucy said.

'Maybe I'm smarter than you. In fact, I know I am. You allowed yourself to get caught. And then you trusted me, this person you'd only just met. You let your craving for sadistic pleasure override caution. I'm not like that. I've learned from your mistakes, Lucy.'

Lucy made a snorting noise.

'I'm a fan, Lucy,' Zoe said. 'I have been since I was a teenager. I'll never forget the first time I saw you on the news and heard about all the things you'd done. Killing those old people. It was something I'd fantasized about for years – but you were brave enough to go there. To do the things I could only dream of.'

Noel couldn't believe what he was hearing. Cool, sporty Zoe, driving around in her little Honda. 'You fantasized about murdering old people?'

'Yes. Well, specifically, my grandparents. They were awful. You should have heard the things they called me. Ugly and fat and stupid. Unfortunately, they both died before I gathered the courage to do what you did, Lucy. But I followed all the trials. I read your book, disappointed that you claimed you were innocent, until I found the secret version. The real version. I've read it over fifty times, Lucy. I've been to the flat where you used to live and stood outside. I've been to Orchard House.' That, Noel knew, was the nursing home where Lucy had worked. 'I breathed in the air where you committed your greatest crimes. I have to admit, when I saw you today, when I spoke to you, I could hardly believe it was happening. They say you should never meet your heroes, don't they? But you didn't disappoint, Lucy. You were, you are, everything I hoped you'd be.'

'So why the hell am I tied up on the floor?' Lucy's voice was a low growl.

'Because I want to be like you, Lucy. I want to be the new you – but an improved version. Lucy two point oh.' She laughed. 'And what's the best way for me to prove that I've transcended your example?'

'By killing her,' Noel said.

'Exactly. The pupil has murdered the master.' Another laugh. 'The rest of the group, your other fans, are going to be so excited and impressed. They'll start to worship me instead. The new Dark Angel.'

'But why us?' Dani asked. Her voice sounded raw – hurt and scared – but with a note of defiance. 'Why did you want to hurt me and Noel?'

'I needed to get Lucy's attention. To win her trust so she would accompany me out of the prison and come here with me. Also, I wanted to see what it would be like, cos-playing as Lucy Newton. Using all her little techniques for ruining people's lives.'

'And?'

'It livened up a very dull month.' She laughed. 'Anyway, I need to get on. I was just going to shoot you, but that's not very Christmassy, is it? I'm going to light this place up – like a Christmas tree!'

She went up the stairs and Noel heard her go through the front door, then come back into the house, her footsteps moving towards the kitchen then back towards the living room. Then he heard her go further upstairs.

'Can you smell that?' Dani asked.

He could. It was petrol.

He struggled with the rope, trying to pull his wrists apart, but Zoe had secured the knot too tightly. They were going to burn to death down here, him and Dani, and they weren't even alone – there was a third party here, a famous psycho, a gooseberry on their final date.

'Why are you laughing?' Dani asked him.

'I didn't know I was.' He tried to get into a sitting position but settled for rolling over so he was facing Dani. Could he smell smoke? Oh God, he could. Zoe had started the fire already.

'I love you, Dani. I want you to remember that. Every day I've spent with you has been amazing, and I was so looking forward to our first Christmas here. You've made me so happy and—'

'Oh, please, shut up!' Lucy said. 'She's coming.'

She was right. Footsteps on the stairs, and then Zoe was back in the basement. The smell of smoke was getting stronger. Where had she started it? On the top floor, he guessed, giving herself time to get out. He remembered something. Mogwai was in the house somewhere. He could see in Dani's eyes that she had already thought about it.

'Please,' Dani said to Zoe. 'Mogwai. Please take her with you.'

Zoe wrinkled her nose. 'Urgh. I don't even like cats.' She looked straight at Lucy. 'I hope you'll think of me as you're burning to death. I'm your legacy. Someone who's learned from you and figured out all the things you could have done better.'

Lucy said something unintelligible.

'What?' Zoe asked.

Lucy said it again, speaking very quietly, her voice a low rumble.

'What are you saying?' Zoe moved towards her, leaning forward.

Lucy leapt up, ankles still bound but her hands free of the rope that had bound them, and Noel saw she was holding the knife he'd taken from the kitchen. He'd forgotten all about it, but he'd been holding it when he fell down the stairs. He must have let go as he landed, the knife skidding within Lucy's reach. She had grabbed it and used it to slowly cut through the rope at her wrists. Noel could see how raw the flesh was there, could imagine how she must have twisted her hands to do it, ignoring the pain. She leapt towards Zoe, plunging the knife into her chest.

Zoe went down, making a horrible gasping noise, and Lucy bent over to cut through the ropes at her feet. The knife was sharp, one of a set Noel had bought when they moved in, and it took less than thirty seconds for her to saw through the rope. Then she stepped straight over the dead Zoe, heading for the steps.

'Wait!' Noel shouted. 'You can't leave us here.'

Lucy paused and turned around. 'I'm Lucy Newton. This is what I do.'

'So do something different. Please, Lucy. We won't tell anyone. We won't ruin your reputation.'

He saw her think about it. Dani was silent, like she was afraid of spooking an animal. Lucy stood there for a few more seconds.

Later, people would speculate that maybe Lucy had learned something by adapting *A Christmas*

Carol. That maybe she feared the fate that befell Marley, wearing the chains she forged in life. Perhaps she felt that by doing one good deed, she might lessen the punishment that was coming her way.

But Noel had looked into her eyes, and he didn't believe any of that. Lucy either did what she did next because she thought it was more interesting, or because she wanted to get one over on Zoe.

She stepped forward and told Noel to turn over. Then she cut through the rope.

As soon as Noel was free, Lucy ran up the stairs and out of sight.

The smell of smoke was much stronger now, but not yet creeping into the basement. Noel focused on his own ankles first, freeing his feet, then crossed to Dani and did the same to the ropes that bound her ankles. Then he helped her to the stairs, stepping over Zoe's body, and they climbed. The smoke was thick in the hallway, the stairway above them ablaze. The heat was intense and Noel knew they had only seconds before the whole downstairs area went up in flames. He pulled Dani towards the front door – trying not to inhale – and heard a miaow.

Mogwai came running out of the kitchen, her

tail puffed up, and Noel scooped her up, scalding the palm of his hand as he turned the handle to open the front door.

They burst out into the night, and Noel collapsed on the lawn, still holding on to the cat, Dani falling to her knees beside him.

He lay on his back and watched the Christmas lights above him sputter and blink, blink again, then go dark.

Epilogue

One Year Later

Noel waited beside the removals truck, the cat carrier at his feet. He was waiting for Dani, who was driving here separately from the temporary accommodation they'd been living in while they waited for their house to be rebuilt. The truck was full of brand-new furniture, and he said a silent prayer of thanks that he had taken out an insurance policy the night of the burglary, even though there were some things they would never get back. The fire had destroyed everything, including their wedding album and Dani's bridal dress, which had been in the wardrobe in their bedroom, along with all the other sentimental items they'd collected during their lives, all the irreplaceable items. They'd lost all their Christmas presents too, including the replacement gifts Noel had bought for Dani.

Really, though, none of that mattered. Because they were still alive. And Noel knew that Zoe had actually done them a favour, in a strange way. He would never take his own life, or Dani's, for granted.

At his feet, Mogwai yowled.

'Yeah, you too,' he said. 'I would have gone back in for you. I promise.'

The removals van driver gave him a look.

He glanced across the street. There was a SOLD sign outside Justin's place. Justin was in jail – not a great fate for a prison officer – for his role in helping Lucy escape. In his house, they'd found files that he'd compiled, including the honest version of her memoir, in which she had confessed to all her crimes and outlined exactly how she felt about other people. It astonished Noel that there were people out there who believed Lucy deserved to be free, that she couldn't help the way she was, or even that she was special. It was as if they looked up to her, like brainwashed sheep worshipping a wolf.

Zoe had pretended to be one of these sheep in order to befriend Justin. At his trial he had confessed that, after meeting Lucy, he had felt there was something special about her, which had led to him researching her online and coming across a private group of people who believed not that she was innocent of her crimes but that she didn't deserve to be punished for them. They thought she was special. Different. Better. Zoe had pretended to be one of those people, so she could get access to Lucy. To get her out so she could enact her warped revenge.

It was a huge story, and Noel and Dani had been right there in the middle of it. The victims of the Christmas Magpie, the nickname Zoe had given herself and that the papers latched on to. They'd had countless offers to tell their story, to describe what it had felt like to encounter the original magpie. To almost die. They had turned it all down, hoping the media would soon get bored and leave them alone, which they eventually did. Noel and Dani also never told anyone, except the police – PC Degville regarding them with open-mouthed scepticism – that Lucy had helped them. He had a feeling Lucy would prefer people not to know.

As he waited for Dani, he saw Linda and Tony coming down the street. They were, and he still couldn't believe this, an item now, though still living separately. If he hadn't known that Zoe had killed Alan, he might have wondered if Tony had done it to remove a love rival.

'Welcome back,' Linda said after hugging him. 'We were going to bring you a little housewarming gift . . .'

'But we figured you'd had enough surprise presents last time you were here,' Tony said. They were already finishing each other's sentences. 'Not to mention the fact that your house has already been thoroughly warmed.'

Noel laughed. 'Dark. But funny.'

'That's me. We were talking about Lucy Newton earlier. Has there been any update?'

'Not that I've heard. The police tell me they will never stop looking for her, but they suspect she's gone abroad. Zoe told us she'd made a plan to get out of the country, and they think Lucy followed that plan. Stealing it from Zoe, basically. But the police haven't managed to find the safe house Zoe talked about or figure out who was helping her. All the people in this online pro-Lucy group deny all knowledge, although of course they are pleased she's free.'

'Well, as long as she never comes back here, I have to say I'm not that bothered,' Linda said. 'I was very impressed by Lucy's adaptation of *A Christmas Carol*, before one of the actors went bonkers at the end and started trying to pull one of the officers' trousers down. Then someone discovered Lucy had escaped and the alarms went off . . . Most eventful Christmas Eve of my life.'

'Ditto,' said Noel. 'With the possible exception of the one when I was born.'

They turned at the sound of a car coming down the street. It pulled over and Dani got out.

'We'll let you two lovebirds get on,' Linda said.

'Again, ditto.'

Linda and Tony walked back up the street towards their houses and Noel picked up Mogwai in his carrier.

'This cat needs to go on a diet,' he said to Dani. 'You've been spoiling him.'

'Okay. But in January. Nobody, man, woman or cat, should be on a diet at Christmas.'

Noel took her hand and they walked to the front door together.

'Here we go,' Dani said. 'Second time lucky?'

'Yep. Two for joy.'

They went inside, though Noel paused on the threshold for a second. This Christmas, Noel was finally going to enjoy himself. He followed Dani into the kitchen, where she had just freed Mogwai from his carrier. There was a bottle of champagne in the car, and some mince pies – shop-bought, guaranteed not to contain chilli powder – in the boot. He was planning to thoroughly indulge himself, watch all his favourite movies and not give a single thought to creepy dolls, Secret Santas or serial killers.

But now, he allowed himself to wonder: where was Lucy? Would they ever find out? He didn't begrudge her her freedom. After all, she had saved their lives, even if it was what any decent human being would do. He wondered if one day, if she ever needed a favour, she would reach out.

He didn't doubt that Lucy would feel they owed her.

Letter from the Author

Thank you for reading *The Christmas Magpie*. I'd love to hear what you thought of it. My email is mark@markedwardsauthor.com or you can follow and contact me on Facebook, Instagram or TikTok. My username on all three is @markedwardsauthor.

On top of that, if you join my newsletter, you'll get a box set of short stories. Just go to www.markedwardsauthor.com/free and sign up.

The Christmas Magpie was designed to work as a standalone, but long-term readers of my books will almost certainly be aware that this is not the first to feature Lucy Newton. However, if this is the first book in the Magpies universe you've read, you can go back and follow Lucy's misadventures from the beginning in this order: *The Magpies*, *A Murder of Magpies*, *Last of the Magpies* and *The Psychopath Next Door*.

Some thanks:

To Stella Newing, who did a brilliant job editing this novella, as well as everyone else at Michael Joseph, including Joel Richardson, Maxine Hitchcock, Ellie Morley and Gaby Young. Thanks, too, to my copy-editor, Sarah Day.

A huge thank you to my fantastic agent Madeleine Milburn, and everyone else at the agency including Valentina, Rachel and Meghan.

The prison sections of this book were partly inspired by visits I made to HMP Thameside and HMP Pentonville. At the latter, I was part of a panel judging a creative writing competition and we were all blown away by the quality of work and enthusiasm of the men who took part. They were taught by Caroline Green, a fantastic author and teacher, who is nothing at all like Camilla!

I should also thank Charles Dickens. I'm sure everyone in the world has either read *A Christmas Carol* or seen one of the many movies, but I highly recommend the audiobook read by Hugh Grant.

This book is dedicated to my sister, Claire Finch, who has had an extremely tough couple of years and does so much for our family. She deserves some good luck, so if everyone sends positive thoughts her way it might just work. It is Christmas, after all.

Finally, thanks to the rest of my family: Mum, Ali, Dad, Jean, all the Baughs, Auntie Jo, Louise and Martin – and, of course, to my extraordinarily clever and beautiful wife, Sara, and to Ellie, Poppy, Archie and Harry. Also, how could I forget Dottie, Sherlock and Willow?

If you made it to the end of this letter – thank you again for reading this book. I hope that, unlike Lucy, you're on Santa's nice list.

Though being naughty can be fun too.

Happy Christmas,

Mark Edwards

If you enjoyed *The Christmas Magpie*, read on for an extract of *The Wasp Trap*

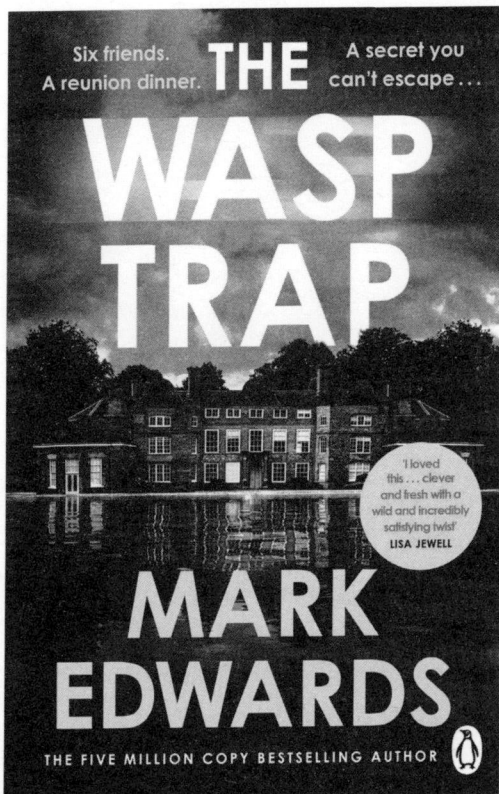

Out now

NURTURING WRITERS SINCE 1935

Prologue

July 1999

It was the last Friday in July and I was trying hard not to panic about the deadline when Lily made the suggestion that would change everything.

'I've had an idea,' she said, in that measured tone of hers. 'I want to devise a test that will tell us if someone is a psychopath.'

There were only three of us left in the library: Lily, Sophie and me. The others had gone outside to smoke or get some air while we carried on working, though at least we were cool in that dark-panelled room that the sun barely touched. The library was now a makeshift office. Antique tables and chairs with wobbly legs had been dragged in from other rooms, and cables snaked across the floorboards to connect the fruit-coloured iMacs that we'd been sitting in front of since first light.

We were spurred on by the date that was written on a whiteboard and propped on a shelf in the fiction section. The launch date, just four weeks away. The fiction section was apt because there was no way the site would be ready by then. But we kept hearing rumours that our rivals were going to beat us to the punch, that *they* would revolutionize online dating, not us. 'No prize for second,' Sebastian kept saying, and we could always tell when he'd been on the phone to his chief investor. He would march into the office, sweat gleaming on his creased brow, and demand to know exactly what we had achieved that day.

'This is our revolution,' he said to us many times. 'We can't let them take it from us.'

I could hear the professor upstairs in his study now, pacing from one end of the room to the other. I looked up. One of the dogs, sitting by my feet, lifted his head too.

'I want to help him,' Lily said, following my gaze towards the ceiling. And that was when she came up with her suggestion. A test to identify psychopaths, a subject I had been obsessed with over the past couple of weeks, since we'd been up there, in Sebastian's study, searching through his papers and scouring the psychology periodicals that he still subscribed to. 'We could ensure it was reliable, trustworthy, something he could use in his other work. What do you think? Will? Sophie?'

A test. Hadn't we done enough of those this summer? I'd been tested before I even met the professor and since coming here, to his house, I'd spent hours in front of the computer, completing questionnaires, trying to figure out how much I agreed or disagreed with statements like *I feel comfortable around strangers*.

'How would you go about it, Lily?'

That was Sophie. She was seated across from me, leaning forward with her elbows on her desk, her wavy black hair tumbling around her face; a face I found it hard not to stare at.

Lily smiled. 'I haven't quite figured that out yet. I'll have to make sure it's not easy to fool.' I could almost hear the crackle of that remarkable brain, the firing of synapses, as she grabbed a pad and pen and began making notes. Sophie and I got up from our desks and peered over Lily's shoulder. She scribbled fast: a flow chart, arrows and question marks. Beyond the library I could hear chatter and laughter.

My colleagues. After a month at the professor's, I was still unsure how many of them I could call friends.

'What do you think?' Lily asked, when she'd finished making notes.

I picked up her notepad and tried to make sense of it. I quickly put it down again. It was like being a work-experience kid on the Manhattan Project.

'Will?'

I chose my words carefully. 'It sounds . . . interesting. And I want to help the professor too. But aren't we busy enough? Everything we're here to do. Our stock options. All of it. We're already running out of time.'

She had the smile of a benevolent dictator. 'It will be fine. I have the capacity, Will. I'll base it on the same algorithm we're using for the site. It's just another form of psychometric testing, really. And if I can't pull it off, we won't have lost anything.' A pause. 'So? Shall we do it?'

I caught Sophie's eye, thinking about another test we'd taken and the results it had spat out, and I wondered if that would ever lead to anything or if work and pressure would get in our way. We still had so many problems that needed fixing. Words that had to be written and polished. Bugs squashed.

I was about to tell Lily we were too busy, that it would be too difficult. A test to catch a psychopath? I had faith in her genius, but did she really have time? And could she really create a test that a psychopath wouldn't be able to fool?

But as I opened my mouth to put forward my argument, Sophie said, 'I'm in. I think it's a brilliant idea. Surely you do too, Will?'

They both turned to me and I swallowed my words.

I simply couldn't say no to them.

'Let's do it,' I said, and both Sophie and Lily clapped their hands.

'What's all the excitement about?'

Georgina came into the room, followed by the others, smelling of cigarettes and sunshine, the spaniel rousing himself and running over to greet them, tail a happy blur. Once everyone was inside, Lily began to tell them about her idea, explaining that we would all need to take part, volunteer to be tested, just as we'd acted as guinea pigs for the dating site.

As they listened to her, the ceiling creaked again. Sebastian, still up there, pacing.

I looked over at my colleagues. Sebastian's six hires and the other two, spending all our time together, sunrise to sunset and sunset to dawn.

No one had protested, not then anyway, although there were one or two frowns of doubt, signs of disquiet that would come out later. At that point, though, there were no arguments, and I knew that, at some point in the coming weeks, we would all risk exposing a darkness in ourselves. A difference.

I looked around again, as the conversation turned towards the evening, to plans, to beer and wine and a dip in the lake. The genius. The lothario. The salesman. The affluent couple, the joker and the local girl. Finally, me, the wordsmith, whose role was to write it all down.

If any of us were a psychopath, I already had a good idea who it would be.

Chapter 1

February 2024

Of course Georgina and Theo lived in an enormous house. Out of all of us, they were the ones who had always been the most likely to achieve success. As individuals, each would have made something of themself, I had no doubt of that. But as a couple? They were unstoppable.

Still, even after the invitation had landed on my doormat and I'd checked the address on Google Maps, I hadn't expected the Howard residence to be quite so impressive. It was a Georgian townhouse, four storeys plus a basement, the last one on a row of imposing terraces in Notting Hill. The house to its left was covered with scaffolding that appeared to have been there some time, green netting flapping in the wind. Next door to the right, set just a little way apart from the row of terraces, was a grand detached house that seemed empty too, its windows dark, the wrought-iron gate secured with a chain and padlock. Between these two unwelcoming buildings the Howards' home stood even prouder and taller, its front windows illuminated, the white paintwork immaculate, a family home that happened to belong to two people I had once known but hadn't seen for over twenty years.

It had taken a death to bring us back together.

You are cordially invited to a dinner party to celebrate the life of
Sebastian Marlowe
Hosted by Theo and Georgina Howard
RSVP

The invitation was printed on thick ivory card, a little grubby at its edges now where I had examined it so many times. Beneath the RSVP was an email address and, on the back, in looping cursive handwriting, a personal message written in blue ink:

> *Dearest Will. Please come! All the old gang will be there and it will be lovely to remember the professor. Can't wait to catch up. G xx*

Catch up. Tell us what you've been up to for the past twenty-five years.

It would take twenty-five seconds.

And it was that thought, picturing Georgina's attempts to suppress the pity she felt for me, that almost sent me back to the tube station, back to my little flat south of the river, where I would spend another evening in front of the TV, waiting for the Deliveroo driver, sharing my dinner with Bernard, my cat – my sole companion since Danielle had left. Bottle of supermarket wine and the optimistic opening of my laptop, the blinking cursor on the blank page.

Waiting for me to tell my story.

That blinking cursor was one of the main reasons I'd accepted the invitation.

'Will?'

The voice, male, came out of the darkness. It was a voice I hadn't heard in a long time but was instantly familiar.

Rohan stepped into the sodium light, brandishing a piece of card that matched mine.

'Mate,' he said. 'I'm so happy to see you. I thought I might be the only one stupid enough to come.'

He grinned as I put out my hand.

'A handshake? Come on, man. Bring it in.' He pulled me into an embrace, patting my back before releasing me and saying, 'You're still as skinny as ever.'

'You're looking good,' I said, though I wasn't sure I meant it. It's always a little depressing to meet up with people you haven't seen in over twenty years; a reminder that youth is a speck in the rear-view mirror. There were dark smudges beneath his eyes, like he'd suffered through a few sleepless nights, and he'd filled out since I'd last seen him. But in other ways, Rohan looked distinguished: his black hair was streaked with silver and he was dressed well. I told him so: 'Looking *sharp*, I should say.'

He held his overcoat open. 'The suit? You like it?' Beneath the streetlight I could see it was midnight blue, well made. 'My brother-in-law's a tailor.'

So he was married. I was going to ask the customary question about whether he had kids – a little later in the evening I would find out that he had two boys, aged nine and eleven, and that he'd been married to Anika for thirteen years – but before I could say anything he let out a whistle as he swivelled on his heels and took in the house.

'Look at this place.' He leaned forward conspiratorially. 'Know how much it's worth?'

He told me. It was the kind of figure that's hard to comprehend, mind-boggling even for London.

'What do they do?' I asked, somehow knowing he would have looked it up. 'For a living, I mean?'

'Theo is in investment banking. Do you remember James? Sebastian's angel investor? Apparently, he gave Theo his first break.' I did remember him. A flash bloke who drove a Porsche and couldn't keep his eyes off Sophie. 'I'm not sure about Georgina, but her family were loaded, weren't they?

7

Probably inherited a fortune. Whatever – can you imagine? Being able to afford a place like this?'

'How do you know *I'm* not loaded? I might have flown here in a gold helicopter.'

He laughed. 'I've been keeping an eye on the bestseller lists, mate. Waiting to see your name. Hasn't happened.'

'Not yet.'

'But when it does you'll be able to afford a gaff like this, right? Maybe a decent suit.'

I tried not to look offended. I was wearing my nicest clothes: a shirt that Danielle had bought me the Christmas-before-last and a smart pair of Levi's. My coat, which had seen me through several wet English winters, was a little thin though, especially in this biting wind.

'Do you know who else is coming?' Rohan asked.

'All the old gang, apparently.' These words, quoted from the back of the invitation, sent a little shiver through my veins.

'Nice. I saw Lily a few years ago at a conference. She's married with kids too. I think she told me her wife is a lawyer.'

'You sound surprised.'

A shrug. 'I never pictured Lily getting married.'

I hadn't either. For someone who had worked for a dating site, Lily had been remarkably uninterested in romance.

'What about Sophie?' I asked, trying to sound casual. 'Do you know what she's up to?'

'Yeah, married to a firefighter. Eight kids.'

'Oh. I never—'

He erupted with laughter. 'Mate, your face. I haven't got a clue what happened to her. She's not on Facebook or anything.'

I already knew she wasn't on social media, not in a way that was easy to trace, anyway. I'd looked for her several times, late at night when I'd had a couple of drinks and started thinking about the past.

'Have you stalked all of us?' I asked.

'Of course. Actually, I sent you a friend request about ten years ago. Guess you never saw it. Or maybe you didn't want to be friends with your old colleague.' He thumped me playfully on the shoulder. 'It's all right, I don't hold grudges.' A wink. 'Much.'

We went up the front steps, Rohan ahead of me. I tried to remember if I'd seen and ignored his friend request. I had no memory of—

A noise stopped me dead.

'Did you hear that?' I asked.

He had reached the top step. 'Hear what?'

I held up a hand. 'Wait.'

We both paused, listening. It had been faint. Muffled. But I was sure I hadn't imagined it. It had sounded like someone crying out. Distressed. Possibly in pain.

'What exactly did you hear?' Rohan asked.

But I didn't get a chance to answer, because the front door opened and there, before me, stood two more people I hadn't seen since the summer of 1999. Theo stepped forward first, pumping Rohan's hand, and then Georgina was there with air kisses, the scent of expensive perfume, her cheek warm against my cold face.

'Just you two?' she said.

'So far.'

'Come in, it's freezing.' Theo gestured for us to go inside.

The three of them went in – Rohan telling Georgina she hadn't aged at all; her half-hearted protests – but I held back, waiting to see if the noise came again.

Cars rushing by on neighbouring streets. The metronome thump of music and a dog barking in the distance. The background hum of London. No cries. No shouts.

I let it go and followed them in.